The Complete Leadership Collection (Vol. 2)

The Book of Five Rings, Tao Te Ching, Self-Reliance & As a Man Thinketh — Classic Guides to Focus, Balance and Inner Authority

A Modern Translation

Adapted for the Contemporary Reader

**Miyamoto Musashi | Lao Tzu
Ralph Waldo Emerson | James Allen**

Translated by Tim Zengerink

Table Of Contents

Preface - Message to the Reader

What If You Could Help Rebuild the Greatest Library in Human History?

Thousands of years ago, the Library of Alexandria stood as the crown jewel of human achievement — a sanctuary where the collected wisdom of every known civilization was gathered, preserved, and shared freely.

And then, it was lost.

Through fire, conquest, and the slow erosion of time, humanity lost not just books — but ideas, dreams, discoveries, and stories that could have changed the world forever.

Today, the Library of Alexandria lives again — and you are invited to be a part of its restoration.

Our mission is simple yet profound:

To rebuild the greatest library the world has ever known, and to translate all timeless works into every language and dialect, so that no seeker of knowledge is ever left behind again.

By joining our movement to rebuild the modern Library of Alexandria, you become part of an unprecedented mission:

- **Unlimited Access to the Greatest Audiobooks & eBooks Ever Written:**

  Instantly explore thousands of legendary works—Plato, Shakespeare, Jane Austen, Leo Tolstoy, and countless more. All instantly available to read or listen, placing a complete literary universe at your fingertips.

- **Beautiful Paperback & Deluxe Editions at Printing Cost**

  Own any title as an elegant paperback, deluxe hardcover, or stunning collectible boxset—offered to you at true printing cost, delivered straight to your door. Build your personal Library of Alexandria, crafted for beauty, built for durability, and worthy of proud display.

- **Fresh Translations for Modern Readers—in Every Language & Dialect**

  Enjoy timeless masterpieces reimagined in clear, contemporary language—no more outdated phrases or obscure references. Alongside the original versions, we're tirelessly translating these classics into every language and dialect imaginable, ensuring accessibility and understanding across cultures and generations.

- **Join a Global Renaissance of Literature & Knowledge**

  You directly support expanding our library, publishing deluxe editions at true cost, translating works into all global languages, and bringing humanity's greatest stories to people everywhere. By joining today, you're not just preserving a legacy of masterpieces; you set in motion a powerful wave of literary accessibility.

Become a Torchbearer of Knowledge.

Join us for free now at **LibraryofAlexandria.com**

Together, we will ensure that the light of human wisdom never fades again.

With gratitude and a shared love of knowledge,
The Modern Library of Alexandria Team

Visit:

www.libraryofalexandria.com

Or scan the code below:

Introduction

Inner Mastery and Outer Influence:
Cultivating Leadership from the Self Outward

The Complete Leadership Collection (Vol. 2) brings together four profound texts that illuminate leadership as an inner art before it becomes an external act. Through The Book of Five Rings by Miyamoto Musashi, Tao Te Ching by Lao Tzu, Self-Reliance by Ralph Waldo Emerson, and the dual works of James Allen—As a Man Thinketh and From Poverty to Power—this volume explores the disciplines of balance, focus, and self-mastery that precede and empower all forms of authentic influence.

Each of these works transcends its cultural or historical context. Though spanning feudal Japan, ancient China, 19th-century America, and the early modern West, they are united by a timeless insight: that true leadership originates from within. Their shared message is simple but revolutionary: control your mind, clarify your purpose, and live with integrity—and your leadership will arise not from effort, but from presence.

This introduction explores the key insights of these texts as a composite guide for leading with clarity, calm, and confidence in an increasingly complex world. Leadership is not merely strategy—it is being. These authors challenge us to lead not by command or coercion, but by example, essence, and inner strength.

Musashi, Lao Tzu, and the Way of Harmony and Discipline

Miyamoto Musashi's The Book of Five Rings is a concise manual of combat strategy written by Japan's most legendary swordsman. Composed in the early 17th century, the book draws from Musashi's personal experiences in over sixty duels and numerous battles. But its teachings extend far beyond the battlefield.

Musashi divides his strategy into five "rings" or elements: Earth, Water, Fire, Wind, and Void. Each ring represents a layer of mastery:

- Earth lays the foundation: stance, discipline, mental readiness.
- Water emphasizes adaptability and flow.
- Fire speaks to aggressive engagement and timing.
- Wind explores the weaknesses of rival schools—learning from others' faults.
- Void is the most elusive: the clarity of no-mind, the wisdom of emptiness.

Musashi's ultimate goal is not brute strength but precision and clarity. He urges the reader to cultivate the "spirit of the thing" and to win without wasting energy. His leadership is not emotional—it is cool, direct, and fully present.

Lao Tzu's Tao Te Ching, written over two millennia earlier, presents a radically different but complementary vision. Rather than the martial way, it offers the path of wu wei—effortless action. The Tao is the source of all things, the flow of the universe, the mystery that cannot be named.

For Lao Tzu, leadership is not about asserting power but embodying balance. The best leaders are invisible; their presence shapes outcomes without control. His central teachings include:

- Yielding is strength. The flexible outlasts the rigid.
- The leader leads by stepping back. Influence flows from emptiness, not from force.
- Act without striving. Let your actions harmonize with the rhythm of the moment.

If Musashi teaches sharpness, Lao Tzu teaches softness. If Musashi calls for discipline, Lao Tzu calls for surrender. Together, they represent the full arc of mastery: active control and passive alignment, strategy and spontaneity.

For modern leaders, these texts offer profound lessons: cultivate inner stillness, observe before reacting, and know when to strike—and when to yield.

Emerson and Allen: Self-Belief, Thought Power, and the Energy of Integrity

Ralph Waldo Emerson's essay Self-Reliance, first published in 1841, is a manifesto for the individual spirit. Writing in the aftermath of the American Revolution and amid industrial expansion, Emerson challenges his readers to abandon conformity, tradition, and fear in favor of direct experience and inner authority.

His central premise: trust thyself. Every person has a unique genius—a divine intuition—that speaks not through books or institutions, but from within. To follow that voice is to risk misunderstanding, ridicule, and solitude. But not to follow it is to betray the soul.

Emerson warns against:

- Consistency, which traps us in outdated roles.
- Society, which pressures us to compromise.
- Tradition, which substitutes memory for vision.

Instead, he urges us to embrace:

- Spontaneity, the expression of divine intuition.
- Boldness, the refusal to seek permission.
- Nonconformity, the prerequisite to greatness.

Self-Reliance is not egoism. It is the courage to follow truth even when it leads away from approval. It is leadership rooted in authenticity, not persuasion.

James Allen, writing at the dawn of the 20th century, expands Emerson's themes into a philosophy of inner causality. In As a Man Thinketh and From Poverty to Power, Allen argues that thought is the seed of all action, character, and destiny. The outer life mirrors the inner world.

His key ideas include:

- Thought shapes reality. We become what we dwell upon.
- Calmness is power. The leader must cultivate peace amid pressure.
- Vision guides action. A strong purpose channels energy.
- Suffering is a signal. It invites reflection and correction.

Allen does not promote wishful thinking—he promotes ethical will. His writing is compact, poetic, and rooted in spiritual principle. He insists that poverty, failure, and weakness are not conditions—but mindsets that can be transformed.

For today's leader, Emerson and Allen offer the interior infrastructure of influence. They teach that clarity, self-trust, and moral vision are the real drivers of sustainable power. They show that public leadership begins with private alignment.

Leading from the Inside Out: An Integrated Philosophy of Presence and Power

These four works—Musashi's swordplay, Lao Tzu's Tao, Emerson's fire, and Allen's quiet resolve—form a circle of leadership that begins and ends in the self. Each, in their own way, insists that before we lead others, we must know how to:

- Master our minds and emotions.
- Clarify our values and vision.
- Act decisively but not reactively.
- Surrender ego and align with deeper laws.

Leadership in the modern age is often confused with image, charisma, or title. But these texts reveal another path: a way of leadership based on integrity, perception, and spiritual depth. They remind us that to influence the world, we must first be unmoved by it.

In crisis, they teach focus. In chaos, balance. In ambition, humility. In success, responsibility. They offer a way of being that does not chase leadership—but attracts it.

Welcome to The Complete Leadership Collection (Vol. 2). May these teachings ground you, guide you, and grow within you the quiet, indestructible force of a true leader.

The Book of Five Rings

Miyamoto Musashi

Introduction

I have spent many years studying the Way of Strategy, known as Ni Ten Ichi Ryu, and now I think it's time to explain it in writing for the first time. It's now early October in the twentieth year of Kanei (1645). I have climbed Mount Iwato in Higo, Kyushu, to pay my respects to heaven, pray to Kwannon, and bow before Buddha. I am a warrior from Harima province, known as Shinmen Musashi No Kami Fujiwara No Genshin, and I am sixty years old. Since I was young, I've been drawn to the Way of Strategy. My first duel was when I was thirteen, where I defeated Arima Kihei, a strategist from the Shinto school. When I was sixteen, I defeated another strategist, Tadashima Akiyama. At twenty-one, I traveled to the capital, facing many strategists, and never lost a single contest. After that, I traveled from province to province, dueling strategists from different schools, and I never lost, even though I had up to sixty matches. This was between the ages of thirteen and twenty-eight or twenty-nine.

When I turned thirty, I reflected on my past victories. They weren't because I had mastered strategy. Maybe it was natural talent, or the will of heaven, or that the other schools' strategies were not as good. After that, I studied day and night, searching for the deeper meaning, and I came to understand the Way of Strategy when I was fifty. Since then, I've lived without following any particular path. Through the virtue of strategy, I have practiced many skills and arts, learning them all without a teacher. When writing this book, I did not rely on the teachings of Buddha, Confucius, or any old war stories or books on martial arts. I pick up my brush to explain the true spirit of this Ichi school, as it reflects the Way of heaven and Kwannon. The time is the night of the tenth day of the tenth month, during the hour of the tiger (3-5 a.m.).

Chapter 1 - The Ground Book

Strategy is the skill of the warrior. Commanders must put this skill into practice, and soldiers should understand this Way. Today, there is no warrior who truly understands the Way of Strategy. There are many Ways to follow. For example, there is the Way of salvation through the teachings of Buddha, the Way of Confucius guiding learning, the Way of healing for doctors, the Way of poets through Waka, and the arts of tea, archery, and many other skills. Each person follows the Way they feel drawn to. It is said that a warrior's Way is the balance between the pen and the sword, and he should have an appreciation for both. Even if someone doesn't have natural talent, they can still be a warrior by dedicating themselves to both sides of the Way.

In general, the Way of the warrior is about accepting death with resolve. Although many people—whether priests, women, peasants, or others—have been known to face death for duty or out of shame, the warrior's focus is different. The study of strategy is about overcoming others. By gaining victory, whether in a duel or in battle, we achieve power and honor for ourselves or our lord. This is the essence of strategy.

In China and Japan, those who follow this Way have been called "masters of strategy." Warriors must learn this Way. Recently, some people have gained fame as strategists, but they are often just sword-fighters. In the past, the attendants of the Kashima and Kantori shrines in Hitachi province received teachings from the gods and established schools that traveled across the land, teaching men. This is the more recent meaning of strategy. In earlier times, strategy was considered one of the Ten Abilities and Seven Arts, recognized as a valuable practice. Although swordsmanship is certainly an art, strategy as a practice was never limited to just the use of the sword.

The true value of swordsmanship goes beyond mere technique. If we look around us, we see that many arts are turned into commodities.

People use their skills to promote themselves. It's as if the nut, the essential part, has become less important than the flower. In this kind of strategy, both teachers and students focus too much on showing off their skills, trying to rush the flower into bloom. They speak of "This Dojo" and "That Dojo," all seeking profit. Someone once said, "Immature strategy causes grief," and that is certainly true.

There are four main paths in life: the paths of the gentleman, the farmer, the artisan, and the merchant. The Way of the farmer is through the use of agricultural tools, observing the changes of the seasons from spring to autumn. The second Way is that of the merchant. A wine maker gathers ingredients and uses them to make his living. The merchant's Way is always to live by seeking profit. This is the Way of the merchant. Third is the gentleman warrior, carrying the tools of his trade. The Way of the warrior is to master the virtue of his weapons. If a gentleman does not care for strategy, he will not see the value in weapons. Shouldn't he at least have a little appreciation for this? Fourth is the Way of the artisan. The Way of the carpenter is to master the use of his tools, first laying out plans with precision, and then following them carefully in his work. This is how he lives his life. These are the four Ways: the gentleman, the farmer, the artisan, and the merchant.

Now, let's compare the Way of the carpenter to strategy. The connection is found in the building of houses. Noble houses, warrior houses, the Four Houses, houses that rise and fall, the style of the house, the traditions of the house, and the reputation of the house all come into play. The carpenter uses a master plan to build, and strategy is similar because there is a plan for a campaign. If you want to learn the art of war, study this book carefully. The teacher is like a needle, and the student is like the thread. You must practice constantly.

Like a chief carpenter, the commander must understand the natural laws, the rules of the land, and the traditions of the people. This is the Way of the chief. The chief carpenter must know the architecture of towers and temples, the plans for palaces, and must direct workers to raise buildings. The Way of the chief carpenter is the same as the commander of a warrior household.

When building, the choice of wood is important. Straight, unblemished timber is used for visible pillars, while straight wood with small flaws is used for interior pillars. Wood that looks good, even if a bit weak, is used for thresholds, lintels, doors, and sliding panels. Strong wood, even if it is knotted or twisted, can still be used discreetly in construction. Timber that is weak throughout is used for scaffolding or later for firewood.

The chief carpenter assigns tasks based on the workers' skills. Some lay floors, others make doors or thresholds, ceilings, and so on. Those with less skill work on floor supports or carve wedges and do smaller tasks. If the chief knows his workers well and uses them wisely, the result will be good. The chief must understand his workers' strengths and weaknesses, keeping morale high and encouraging them when needed. This is the same principle found in strategy.

Like a warrior, a carpenter sharpens his own tools. He carries his equipment in a toolbox and works under the direction of the foreman. He uses an axe to make columns and girders, a plane to shape floorboards and shelves, and cuts fine details as accurately as his skill allows. This is the craft of carpentry. When a carpenter becomes skilled and understands measurements, he can become a foreman. His accomplishments range from making small shrines and writing shelves to tables, lanterns, chopping boards, and pot lids. These are the specialties of a skilled carpenter.

Things are similar for the soldier. You should think deeply about this. The carpenter's skill is in making sure that his work doesn't warp, that the joints fit properly, and that everything is perfectly planed so it all fits together well, not just in parts. This is essential. If you want to learn this Way, carefully study the things written in this book, one at a time. You must research thoroughly.

This Book of Strategy is divided into five sections, each focusing on different aspects: Ground, Water, Fire, Wind (tradition), and Void (the illusory nature of worldly things). The foundation of the Way of Strategy, from the perspective of my Ichi school, is explained in the Ground book. It's difficult to fully understand the true Way by focusing only on sword-fighting. You must understand both the smallest and the largest things, the most shallow and the deepest things. As if the Way were a straight road mapped on the ground, the first section is called the Ground book.

The second section is the Water book. With water as the theme, the spirit should become like water. Water takes the shape of whatever it is in; sometimes it flows gently, other times it crashes like the sea. Water has a clear, blue color. Through clarity, the teachings of the Ichi school are revealed in this book. If you master the principles of sword-fighting, when you can defeat one man, you can defeat any man in the world. The spirit of defeating one person is the same as defeating many. A strategist can make small things into big things, like building a great Buddha from a small model. I cannot explain in full detail how this is done, but the principle of strategy is to know one thing in order to know ten thousand things. The principles of the Ichi school are explained in the Water book.

The third section is the Fire book. This book is about combat. The spirit of fire is fierce, whether it is a small flame or a large one; the same goes for battles. The way of fighting is the same whether it's a one-on-one duel or a battle with ten thousand soldiers. You must understand that a spirit can be large or small. What is large is easy to see; what is small is harder to notice. For large groups of people, it's hard to change positions, so their movements can be predicted. But an individual can change his mind easily, making his actions harder to foresee. You must grasp this. The key to this section is that you must train day and night to make quick decisions. In strategy, training should become part of daily life, and your spirit should remain steady. This section on combat is explained in the Fire book.

The fourth section is the Wind book. This part does not focus on my Ichi school, but on other schools of strategy. By Wind, I mean old traditions, present-day traditions, and family traditions in strategy. I explain the strategies of the world clearly here. This is tradition. It is hard to know yourself if you don't understand others. Every Way has side paths. If you study a Way every day and your spirit strays, you might think you're following the right path, but in reality, it is not the true Way. If you follow the true Way but stray just a little, over time, this small deviation will turn into a large one. You must recognize this. Other strategies have come to focus too much on sword-fighting, and it's understandable that this happened. However, my strategy's true value lies in a different principle, though it includes sword-fighting. I explain what strategy means in other schools in the Wind book.

The fifth section is the Void book. By Void, I mean that which has no beginning and no end. To grasp this principle means not grasping it at all. The Way of Strategy is the Way of nature. When you understand the power of nature and the rhythm of every situation, you will naturally know how to strike the enemy. This is the Way of the Void. I aim to show how to follow the true Way, according to nature, in the Void book.

The name "Ichi Ryu Ni To" means "One school, two swords." Warriors, both commanders and soldiers, carry two swords at their belts. In earlier times, these were called the long sword and the short sword. Today, they are known as the sword and the companion sword.Let it be enough to say that, in our country, for whatever reason, a warrior carries two swords at his belt. This is the Way of the warrior. "Nito Ichi Ryu" shows the advantages of using both swords. The spear and halberd are weapons used outdoors. Students of the Ichi school Way of Strategy should start training with a sword in one hand and a long sword in the other. This is a truth: when you are ready to sacrifice your life, you must make the fullest use of your weapons. It is wrong not to do so and to die without even drawing a weapon.

If you hold a sword with both hands, it's harder to swing it freely to the left and right. That's why my method is to carry the sword in one hand. This doesn't apply to large weapons like spears or halberds, but swords and companion swords can be used with one hand. Holding a sword with both hands can be a burden when you're on horseback, running over rough roads, swampy ground, muddy rice fields, stony paths, or in a crowd of people. Using both hands to hold the long sword isn't the true Way because if you're carrying a bow, spear, or other weapons in your left hand, you'll only have one hand free for the long sword. However, when it's too hard to strike an enemy down with one hand, you should use both hands.

It isn't hard to wield a sword with one hand; the Way to learn this is by training with two long swords, one in each hand. It will seem difficult at first, but everything is difficult in the beginning. Bows are hard to draw, halberds are hard to use, but as you practice with the bow, your pull becomes stronger. As you get used to handling the long sword, you will gain power and skill with it. As I will explain in the Water Book, there is no quick method to mastering the long sword. The long sword should be used in broad strokes, and the companion sword should be used in close combat. This is the first thing to understand.

According to the Ichi school, you can win with a long weapon, but you can also win with a short one. In short, the Way of the Ichi school is the spirit of victory, no matter what weapon you use or its size. It's better to use two swords rather than one when fighting a crowd, especially if you want to take a prisoner. These things are hard to explain in detail. From one thing, you can learn ten thousand things. When you truly understand the Way of Strategy, nothing will be hidden from you. You must study hard.

The Meaning of the Two Characters for "Strategy"

Masters of the long sword are called strategists. In other military arts, those who master the bow are called archers, those who master the spear are spearmen, those who master the gun are marksmen, and those who master the halberd are halberdiers. But we don't call masters of the long sword "longswordsmen" or "companion swordsmen." Since bows, guns, spears, and halberds are part of a warrior's equipment, they are certainly part of strategy. To master the long sword is to govern oneself and the world. The principle is "strategy by means of the long sword." If someone masters the long sword, one man can defeat ten. And just as one man can defeat ten, one hundred can defeat one thousand, and one thousand can defeat ten thousand. In my strategy, one man is equal to ten thousand, making this strategy the complete skill of the warrior.

The Way of the warrior does not include other Ways like Confucianism, Buddhism, certain traditions, artistic accomplishments, or dancing. But even though these are not part of the Way, if you understand the Way broadly, you will see it reflected in everything. Men must polish their own Way.

The Benefit of Weapons in Strategy

There is a time and place for using different weapons. The best use of the companion sword is in tight spaces or when you are engaged closely with an opponent. The long sword is effective in almost any situation. The halberd, however, is not as good as the spear on the battlefield. The spear gives you the advantage to attack first, while the halberd is more defensive. Between two men of equal skill, the spear offers a slight edge. Both the spear and the halberd have their uses, but neither works well in confined spaces, nor are they good for capturing prisoners. They are mainly for open battlefields.

If you focus too much on "indoor" techniques, you will think too narrowly and forget the true Way, making real-life encounters more difficult. The bow is useful at the start of a battle, especially in open areas like moors, where you can shoot quickly among the spearmen. But the bow is less useful during sieges or when the enemy is farther than forty yards away. For this reason, there are fewer traditional schools of archery today, as this skill is less needed now.

Within fortifications, the gun is unmatched. It is the best weapon before the lines of battle meet, but once swords are drawn, the gun becomes useless. One advantage of the bow is that you can see the arrows in flight and correct your aim, whereas with gunfire, the shots cannot be seen. You must understand the importance of this.

Just as a horse needs endurance and should be free from defects, so too must weapons be strong and reliable. Horses should walk with strength, and swords and companion swords should cut with strength. Spears and halberds must be able to endure heavy use, and bows and guns must be sturdy. Weapons should be tough, not just decorative. You should not favor any particular weapon. Becoming overly attached to one weapon is just as bad as not knowing it well enough. You should not simply imitate others, but use weapons that you can handle well. It's not good for commanders or soldiers to have preferences or aversions when it comes to weapons. These are things you must learn deeply.

Timing in Strategy

There is timing in everything. Mastering timing in strategy requires a great deal of practice. Timing is important in dancing and playing musical instruments like the flute or the lute because rhythm only works if the timing is correct. The same applies to military arts, shooting bows or guns, and riding horses. Every skill and ability involves timing. There is even timing in the Void. Timing governs the entire life of a warrior, from his rise and fall, his harmony and discord. Similarly, timing plays a role in the merchant's life, with the rise and fall of capital. Everything follows a rhythm of rising and falling, and you must learn to recognize this.

In strategy, there are many types of timing. From the beginning, you must know the difference between applicable timing and inapplicable timing. You must also understand the timing of large and small things, as well as fast and slow actions, finding the right timing by first recognizing distance and the background timing. This is the key to strategy. Knowing the background timing is especially important; without it, your strategy will become unstable. You win battles by mastering the timing of the Void, which comes from knowing your enemy's timing and using a rhythm they do not expect.

All five books focus primarily on timing. You must train diligently to truly understand this.

If you practice day and night with the Ichi school's strategy, your spirit will naturally grow. In this way, large-scale strategy and hand-to-hand combat strategy will spread throughout the world. This has been written down for the first time in the five books of Ground, Water, Fire, Wind (Tradition), and Void.

This is the way for those who want to learn my strategy:

1. Do not think dishonestly.
2. The Way is in training.
3. Become familiar with every art.
4. Know the Ways of all professions.
5. Understand the difference between gain and loss in worldly matters.
6. Develop intuitive judgment and understanding for all things.
7. Perceive the things that cannot be seen.
8. Pay attention to even the smallest details.
9. Do nothing that is useless.

It is important to start by placing these broad principles in your heart and train in the Way of Strategy. If you don't look at things from a wide perspective, it will be difficult to master strategy. If you learn and master this strategy, you will never lose, even when facing twenty or thirty opponents.

Most importantly, you must set your heart on strategy and follow the Way with great dedication. Once you do this, you will be able to defeat men in real combat and win with just a glance. With enough training, you will be able to control your body freely, conquer men with your physical presence, and eventually, with enough spirit, defeat ten men at once. When you reach this level, wouldn't that make you invincible?

Furthermore, in large-scale strategy, a superior man will manage many subordinates skillfully, carry himself with proper conduct, govern a country, and care for the people, thus maintaining the ruler's discipline. If there is a Way that involves never being defeated, helping oneself, and gaining honor, it is the Way of Strategy.

Chapter 2 - The Water Book

The spirit of the Ni Ten Ichi school of strategy is based on water, and this Water Book explains methods of victory using the long sword of the Ichi school. Language alone cannot fully describe the Way in detail, but it can be grasped intuitively. Study this book carefully; read a word, then reflect deeply on its meaning. If you interpret the teachings too loosely, you will misunderstand the Way. The principles of strategy written here are expressed in terms of one-on-one combat, but you must think broadly enough to apply them to battles involving ten thousand men. Strategy is different from other practices in that if you stray even slightly from the Way, you will become confused and follow the wrong path.

Simply reading this book will not lead you to the Way of Strategy. You must absorb the ideas within these pages. Do not just read, memorize, or copy; rather, study with dedication so that you come to understand the principles from deep within your own heart and incorporate them into your body.

Spiritual Bearing in Strategy

In strategy, your spiritual bearing should not differ from your normal state. Both in combat and in daily life, you should be calm yet determined. Face situations without tension, but also without carelessness, maintaining a settled spirit that is free from bias. Even when your spirit is calm, do not let your body relax, and when your body is relaxed, keep your spirit alert. Do not let your spirit be controlled by your body, or let your body be controlled by your spirit. Avoid being either too passive or overly intense. A spirit that is too high is weak, and a spirit that is too low is also weak. Do not allow the enemy to sense your spirit.

Smaller individuals must understand the spirit of larger people, and larger individuals must be familiar with the spirit of smaller people. Regardless of your size, do not be misled by your own body's reactions. Keep your spirit open and unrestricted, and view things from a higher perspective. You must cultivate your wisdom and spirit. Sharpen your wisdom by learning public justice, distinguishing between good and evil, and studying various arts one by one. When you reach the point where you cannot be deceived by others, you will have realized the wisdom of strategy. The wisdom of strategy is unique. Even in the heat of battle, when you are under great pressure, you must continuously research the principles of strategy to develop a steady, unwavering spirit.

Stance in Strategy

Take a stance with your head held upright—not drooping, not tilted upward, and not twisted. Your forehead and the space between your eyes should remain relaxed, with no wrinkles. Do not roll your eyes or allow them to blink too often, but keep them slightly narrowed. Maintain a composed expression, keeping your nose aligned straight, and feel a slight flare in your nostrils. Keep the back of your neck straight, infusing energy into your hairline, and let this vigor extend down through your whole body from your shoulders.

Lower your shoulders without sticking out your buttocks. Focus your strength in your legs, from your knees down to your toes. Keep your abdomen braced so that you don't bend at the hips. Wedge your companion sword firmly against your abdomen, ensuring that your belt is not loose—this is known as "wedging in." In all aspects of strategy, it is important to maintain your combat stance in everyday life and make your everyday stance your combat stance. Research this deeply.

The Gaze in Strategy

Your gaze should be large and expansive. This is the twofold gaze, "Perception and Sight." Perception is strong, while sight is weak. In strategy, it is crucial to see distant things as if they were near and to view close things from a distanced perspective. In strategy, it's important to focus on the enemy's sword and not get distracted by small, unimportant movements. You must study this carefully. The gaze used in single combat is the same as in large-scale strategy. In strategy, you must learn to look to both sides without moving your eyes. You cannot master this skill quickly. Learn what is written here, and use this gaze in everyday life without changing it, no matter what happens.

Holding the Long Sword

Hold the long sword with a relaxed grip, using a light touch with your thumb and forefinger, while keeping the middle finger neither too tight nor too loose, and the last two fingers tightly. It's bad to have too much play in your hands. When you take up the sword, your mindset should be focused on cutting the enemy. As you strike, don't change your grip, and don't let your hands tremble. When you deflect the enemy's sword, or block or press it down, slightly adjust the pressure in your thumb and forefinger. Above all, maintain the intent to cut the enemy through the way you grip the sword. The grip for combat and for testing swords is the same. There is no separate "man-cutting grip." Generally, I dislike stiffness in both swords and hands. Stiffness means a dead hand, while flexibility means a living hand. Keep this in mind.

Footwork

Walk with the tips of your toes lightly touching the ground, while stepping firmly with your heels. Whether you move quickly or slowly, with large or small steps, your feet should move naturally, as if walking normally. I dislike the three footwork methods known as "jumping foot," "floating foot," and "fixed steps." The so-called "Yin-Yang foot" is important in this Way. It means not moving only one foot. It involves moving your feet left-right and right-left when cutting, stepping back, or deflecting a strike. You shouldn't favor one foot over the other.

The Five Attitudes

The five attitudes are: Upper, Middle, Lower, Right Side, and Left Side. These are the five. Although there are five different positions, the purpose of all of them is to cut the enemy. These are the only five attitudes. No matter what position you're in, don't focus on forming the attitude; just think about cutting. Your stance should be large or small depending on the situation. The Upper, Lower, and Middle attitudes are decisive, while the Left and Right Side attitudes are flexible. Use Left or Right attitudes when there's something in the way overhead or to the side. The decision to use Left or Right depends on the situation.

The key to understanding attitude lies in mastering the middle attitude. The middle attitude is the core of all the attitudes. If we think of strategy on a larger scale, the Middle attitude is like the leader, and the other four attitudes follow the leader. You must grasp this concept.

The Way of the Long Sword

Knowing the Way of the long sword means being able to wield the sword you usually carry with just two fingers. If you understand the path of the sword, you'll be able to handle it easily. If you try to wield the long sword too quickly, you'll lose sight of the Way. To use the long sword properly, you must handle it calmly. If you try to use it like a fan or a short sword, you'll make the mistake of "short sword chopping." You cannot strike down an enemy with a long sword this way.

After you swing the long sword downward, lift it back up straight. When you swing it sideways, return it along the same path. Always return the sword in a controlled manner, keeping your elbows stretched broadly. Wield the sword with strength. This is the Way of the long sword. If you learn to use the five approaches in my strategy, you will handle the sword well. You must train constantly.

The Five Approaches

The first approach is the Middle attitude. Face the enemy with the tip of your sword aimed at his face. When he attacks, deflect his sword to the right and "ride" it. Alternatively, when the enemy attacks, hit the tip of his sword downward, hold your long sword in place, and when he attacks again, cut his arms from below. This is the first method. The five approaches are like this. You must train repeatedly with the long sword to learn them. When you master my Way of the long sword, you'll be able to control any attack the enemy makes. I guarantee there are no other attitudes beyond the five attitudes of the Ni To long sword.

In the second approach with the long sword, from the Upper attitude, cut the enemy just as he attacks. If the enemy dodges your cut, keep your sword in place and, as he comes in again, cut him from below. You can repeat the cut from this position. In this approach, there are different variations of timing and spirit. You will understand this through training in the Ichi school. You will always win with the five long sword methods. You must train repeatedly.

In the third method, take the Lower stance, preparing to scoop upward. When the enemy attacks, strike his hands from below. He may try to knock your sword down, and if he does, cut his upper arm(s) horizontally, as if "crossing" his attack. This technique involves hitting the enemy at the moment he attacks from the lower stance. You will encounter this often, both as a beginner and later in strategy. You must train with the long sword.

In the fourth method, take the Left Side stance. When the enemy attacks, strike his hands from below. If he tries to knock your sword down, parry his attack and cut across from above your shoulder. This is the Way of the long sword. You win by deflecting the enemy's attack. You must study this technique.

In the fifth method, use the Right Side stance. As the enemy attacks, move your long sword from below to the Upper stance, then cut straight down. This technique is crucial for mastering the long sword. Once you understand this method, you will be able to handle a heavy long sword with ease.

I cannot describe every detail of these five methods. You must become familiar with the "in harmony with the long sword" technique, learn the large-scale timing, understand the enemy's long sword, and practice the five methods from the start. You will always win using these techniques, considering timing and the enemy's intentions. Think carefully about all this.

The "Attitude No-Attitude" Teaching

"Attitude No-Attitude" means there is no need for set long sword stances. However, attitudes do exist as the five ways of holding the long sword. No matter how you hold the sword, it should be in a way that makes it easy to cut the enemy, based on the situation, the place, and your relation to the enemy. From the Upper stance, if your spirit lowers, you can move to the Middle stance. From the Middle stance, you can lift the sword slightly and return to the Upper stance. From the Lower stance, you can raise the sword to adopt the Middle stance as needed.

Depending on the situation, if you move the sword from either the Left or Right Side stance toward the center, you can shift to the Middle or Lower stance. This principle is called "Existing Attitude - Nonexisting Attitude." The most important thing when holding a sword is your intention to cut the enemy, no matter what. Whenever you parry, strike, leap, or touch the enemy's sword, your movement must carry through to cutting the enemy. This is essential. If you only think about hitting, leaping, or striking, you won't be able to cut him. Above all, you must focus on completing the movement by cutting the enemy. You must research this thoroughly.

In large-scale strategy, attitude is referred to as "Battle Array." These stances are all for winning battles. Fixed formations are ineffective. Study this deeply.

To Hit the Enemy "In One Timing"

"In One Timing" means, when you have closed the distance with the enemy, strike him as quickly and directly as possible, without adjusting your body or spirit, while you see that he is still uncertain. The timing of striking before the enemy decides to retreat, block, or strike is the "In One Timing." You must train to achieve this instant timing.

The "Abdomen Timing of Two"

When you attack and the enemy retreats quickly, as you notice him tense up, feint a strike. Then, when he relaxes, follow through and hit him. This is called the "Abdomen Timing of Two." It is hard to fully grasp this through reading alone, but with a little instruction, you will soon understand.

No Design, No Conception

In this method, when the enemy attacks and you also decide to attack, strike with your body, spirit, and sword, moving quickly and strongly from the Void. This is the "No Design, No Conception" strike. It is the most important method of striking and is often used. You must train diligently to understand it.

The Flowing Water Cut

The "Flowing Water Cut" is used when you are locked blade to blade with the enemy. When the enemy pulls back and tries to spring at you with his long sword, expand your body and spirit, and cut him slowly with your long sword, like water flowing steadily. If you master this, you can cut with certainty. You must understand the enemy's level of skill.

Continuous Cut

When you attack and the enemy also strikes, and your swords clash together, in one motion, cut his head, hands, and legs. Cutting multiple parts in one sweep of the long sword is the "Continuous

Cut." You must practice this cut often; it is frequently used. With detailed training, you will understand it.

The Fire and Stones Cut

The "Fire and Stones Cut" means that when your long sword clashes with the enemy's, you cut as forcefully as possible without raising the sword at all. This involves cutting quickly with the hands, body, and legs—all three working together with strength. With enough practice, you will strike powerfully.

The Red Leaves Cut

The "Red Leaves Cut" refers to knocking down the enemy's long sword. Your spirit should aim to control his sword. When the enemy is in a long sword stance and intends to cut, hit, or parry, you strike his sword hard using the "Fire and Stones Cut," perhaps with the same spirit as the "No Design, No Conception" Cut. If you beat down his sword with a sticky feeling, he will drop his sword. With enough practice, this cut will allow you to disarm the enemy.

The Body in Place of the Long Sword

Also known as "the long sword in place of the body." Normally, we move our bodies and swords together to strike the enemy. However, depending on the enemy's cutting technique, you can strike him first with your body and then follow with the sword. If the enemy's body is immobile, you can cut first with the long sword, but usually, you strike with your body first and then cut with the long sword. You must study this carefully and practice your strikes.

Cut and Slash

Cutting and slashing are two different things. Cutting is decisive, and it must be done with a determined spirit. Slashing is just making contact with the enemy. Even if you slash powerfully, and the enemy dies immediately, it's still just a slash. When you cut, your spirit must be fully committed. You must understand this. If you first slash the enemy's hands or legs, you must follow up with a strong cut. Slashing, in spirit, is the same as touching. Once you realize this, they will feel similar. Learn this lesson well.

Chinese Monkey's Body

The Chinese Monkey's Body refers to the spirit of not extending your arms. The idea is to close in on the enemy quickly, without fully stretching out your arms, before the enemy has a chance to cut. By keeping your arms from stretching out, you effectively create more distance. The spirit is to advance with your entire body. When you're within arm's reach, it becomes easier to move your body in. Study this well.

Glue and Lacquer Emulsion Body

The "Glue and Lacquer Emulsion Body" is about sticking to the enemy and not separating from him. When you approach, you should connect firmly with your head, body, and legs. Many people advance with their head and legs quickly but let their body lag behind. You should stick firmly so that there is no gap between your body and the enemy's. Think about this carefully.

To Strive for Height

"To strive for height" means that when you close in on the enemy, you should aim to gain the upper position without shrinking back. Stretch your legs, hips, and neck to face the enemy. When you feel that you have gained the upper position, push forward strongly. Learn this method.

To Apply Stickiness

When the enemy attacks and you respond with your long sword, approach with a sticky feeling, holding your long sword against his as you receive his cut. Stickiness doesn't mean hitting hard, but rather making sure the swords don't separate easily. It's best to approach calmly when using this technique. Stickiness is firm, while entanglement is weak. Learn the difference.

The Body Strike

The Body Strike is when you advance through a gap in the enemy's defense and strike him with your body. Turn your face slightly to the side and strike the enemy's chest with your left shoulder pushed forward. Approach with the spirit of bouncing the enemy away, timing your strike with your breath. If you master this method, you will be able to push the enemy back several feet. It's possible to strike with enough force to kill. Train well.

Three Ways to Parry His Attack

There are three ways to parry a cut: First, when the enemy attacks, push his long sword to your right, as if aiming for his eyes. Or, parry by pushing his sword toward his right eye with the feeling of slicing his neck. Lastly, if your long sword is short, close in on him quickly without worrying about parrying, and thrust at his face with your left hand. You should also remember that you can clench your left hand into a fist and strike at his face. Train hard to master these methods.

To Stab at the Face

To stab at the face means that when you are confronting the enemy, your intent should be on stabbing at his face, following the line of your blades with the tip of your long sword. When you aim for the face, the enemy's body will become more vulnerable. When the enemy's body becomes open, there are many chances to win. Keep your focus on this technique. When the enemy becomes exposed, you can win quickly, so don't forget to stab at the face. Train to understand this fully.

To Stab at the Heart

To stab at the heart means that when there are obstacles above or to the sides, and it's hard to cut, thrust directly at the enemy's chest. You must stab him without letting the tip of your long sword waver, showing the ridge of the blade to the enemy while pushing forward with the spirit of deflecting his sword. This method is helpful when you're tired or when your sword is not cutting properly. Understand this technique well.

To Scold "Tut-TUT!"

"Scold" means that when the enemy tries to counterattack as you strike, you cut again from below, as if thrusting, to pin him down. With quick timing, you cut while scolding the enemy. Thrust up with a "Tut!" and cut with a "TUT!" This timing happens often in the exchange of blows. To "scold Tut-TUT" is to time the cut with raising your long sword, as if to thrust. You must practice this frequently to learn it.

The Smacking Parry

The "smacking parry" is when you clash swords with the enemy, meeting his attack with a rhythm of "tee-dum, tee-dum," smacking his sword and cutting him. The point of the smacking parry is not to parry or hit strongly but to match the enemy's attack and quickly cut him. If you understand the timing of smacking, no matter how hard your swords clash, your sword's point will not be knocked back. Train to master this timing.

There are Many Enemies

"There are many enemies" refers to fighting against multiple opponents. Draw both your sword and companion sword and take a wide stance, with your swords covering both sides. The strategy is to chase the enemies around, even if they come from all directions. Watch their order of attack and respond first to those who attack first. Sweep your eyes around, assess their positions, and cut to the left and right with your swords. Don't wait too long. Always return to your stance quickly and cut the enemies down as they approach, crushing them from whichever direction they attack. Keep driving the enemies together, like lining up a row of fish, and when they bunch up, cut them down strongly without giving them a chance to move.

The Advantage when Coming to Blows

You can learn how to win with the long sword through strategy, but it can't be fully explained in writing. You must practice hard to understand how to win.

Oral tradition: "The true Way of Strategy is revealed in the long sword."

One Cut

You can win with certainty through the spirit of "one cut." It's difficult to achieve this without mastering strategy. But if you train well in this Way, strategy will come from within you, and you will be able to win at will. You must train diligently.

Direct Communication

The spirit of "Direct Communication" is how the true Way of the Ni To Ichi school is passed down.

Oral tradition: "Teach your body strategy.

This book outlines the sword-fighting of the Ichi school. To win using the long sword in strategy, first learn the five approaches and the five attitudes. Let the Way of the long sword become natural to your body. Understand spirit and timing, handle the long sword naturally, and move your body and legs in harmony with your spirit. Whether you are fighting one person or two, you will learn the values of strategy. Study the contents of this book, one concept at a time, and by fighting against enemies, you will gradually understand the principles of the Way.

Be patient and deliberate, absorbing the virtue of all this. When you face an enemy, maintain this spirit. Step by step, walk the thousand-mile road. Study strategy over many years and achieve the spirit of the warrior. Today, you must defeat the version of yourself from yesterday; tomorrow, you will defeat lesser men.

To defeat more skilled opponents, train according to this book, and do not let your heart stray from the path. Even if you kill an enemy, if it's not based on what you've learned, it's not the true Way. If you master this Way of victory, you will be able to defeat dozens of men. What remains is to refine your sword-fighting ability, which you will gain through battles and duels.

Chapter 3 - The Fire Book

In this book of the Ni To Ichi school of strategy, I describe fighting like fire. First, people tend to think too narrowly about strategy. They use only the tips of their fingers and understand just a small part of what their whole wrist can do. They let a fight be decided, like using a folding fan, with only the span of their forearms. They focus on small things like hand and leg movements, practicing with a bamboo sword.

In my strategy, learning to defeat enemies comes through many battles, fighting to survive, discovering the meaning of life and death, learning the way of the sword, judging the power of attacks, and understanding the "edge and ridge" of the sword. You can't rely on small tricks, especially when wearing full armor. My way of strategy is the sure way to win when fighting for your life, whether you're facing one person or five or ten. There's nothing wrong with the idea that "one man can defeat ten, and so a thousand can beat ten thousand." You need to study this. Of course, you can't gather a thousand or ten thousand men for daily training. But by training alone with a sword, you can master strategy, understand the enemy's tactics, their strength, and resources, and learn how to defeat ten thousand enemies.

Anyone who wants to master my strategy must study hard, practicing every morning and evening. This is how you refine your skill, let go of your ego, and achieve extraordinary ability. Eventually, you will gain incredible power. This is the practical outcome of strategy.

Depending on the Place

Pay attention to your surroundings. Stand in the sunlight; this means positioning yourself with the sun at your back. If that's not possible, keep the sun on your right side. Indoors, stand with the entrance behind you or to your right. Make sure your back is clear, and that there is open space to your left, with your right side occupied by your stance. At night, if the enemy is visible, keep any light source behind you, with the entrance to your right, and otherwise follow the same rules as before. You should be positioned slightly higher than your enemy. For instance, the Kamiza in a house is considered a high place. In battle, always try to force the enemy to your left. Push them into difficult spots and keep them in awkward positions with their back to those places. Once the enemy is in a bad spot, don't let them look around, but keep pressing them and pin them down. Inside buildings, force them into thresholds, lintels, doors, verandas, or pillars, again preventing them from understanding their situation. Always move the enemy into bad footing or obstacles and use the advantages of the location to gain a better fighting position. You need to study and practice this thoroughly.

The Three Methods to Forestall the Enemy

The first method is to attack first. This is called Ken No Sen (taking the initiative). Another method is to strike as the enemy attacks. This is called Tai No Sen (waiting for the right moment). The last method is to attack at the same time as the enemy. This is called Tai Tai No Sen (matching the enemy's attack and countering). These are the only three ways to take the lead in a fight. Winning quickly by taking the lead is one of the most important aspects of strategy. There are several factors in taking the lead. You need to make the most of the situation, understand the enemy's intentions, and defeat them. This is something that cannot be fully explained in writing.

Ken No Sen

When you choose to attack, stay calm and rush in quickly, taking the initiative before the enemy can react. Alternatively, you can approach with strength but keep your mind focused, taking the lead while remaining composed. Or, you can advance with as much power as possible and, when you reach the enemy, move a little faster than usual with your feet, disrupting and overpowering them sharply. Another option is to attack with a calm spirit, but with the feeling that you're crushing the enemy completely, from start to finish. The spirit is to win deep within the enemy. These are all examples of Ken No Sen.

Tai No Sen

When the enemy attacks, stay composed but pretend to be weak. As the enemy comes near, move away as if you're going to step aside, then quickly rush in and attack strongly when you see the enemy let their guard down. Another way is to attack even harder when the enemy strikes, using the confusion in their timing to win. This is the principle of Tai No Sen.

Tai Tai No Sen

When the enemy attacks quickly, you must attack strongly and calmly, aiming for their weak point as they approach, and defeat them forcefully. Or, if the enemy attacks more cautiously, watch their movements closely and, with your body somewhat light, mirror their movements as they approach. Then move swiftly and cut them down forcefully. This is Tai Tai No Sen. These ideas are hard to explain fully with words. You must study what is written here.

In these three methods of forestalling, you must assess the situation carefully. This doesn't mean you always need to attack first, but if the enemy does attack first, you can still take control. In strategy, once you can anticipate the enemy's moves, you've already gained the upper hand, so you must train well to reach this point.

To Hold Down a Pillow

"To Hold Down a Pillow" means keeping the enemy from rising up. In strategy, it's a mistake to be led around by the enemy. You should always aim to be the one leading the enemy. Of course, the enemy will also try to lead you, but they can't do that if you prevent them from making their move. In strategy, you must block the enemy's attempts to strike, push back against their thrusts, and counter when they try to grapple. That's what "to hold down a pillow" means. Once you understand this concept, you'll be able to see what the enemy is planning before they can act, and stop them. The key is to cut off their attack at the very start: stop them right when they think about attacking. The most important thing in strategy is to block the enemy's useful actions but allow their useless ones. However, if you only block, that's defensive. You must also act according to the Way, stopping the enemy's techniques, ruining their plans, and then taking full control. When you can do this, you'll be a master of strategy. You must train hard and study "holding down a pillow."

Crossing at a Ford

"Crossing at a ford" is like crossing the sea at a narrow point, or sailing across a broad stretch of ocean at a crossing place. I believe we often face "crossing at a ford" moments in life. It means setting out even when your friends stay behind, knowing the way, trusting your ship, and recognizing that the day is in your favor. When everything lines up—maybe with a favorable wind—then you set sail. But if the wind changes just before you reach your goal, you'll have to row the rest of the way. This mindset applies to daily life as well. You should always think about crossing at a ford. In strategy, it's also important to "cross at a ford." Assess the enemy's strengths and weaknesses, understand your own, and attack at the best point, like a skilled captain choosing the right sea route. If you cross at the most favorable point, you can relax afterward. Crossing at a ford means striking at the enemy's weak spot and putting yourself in an advantageous position. This is how to win in large-scale strategy. The spirit of crossing at a ford is important in both large and small strategies. You must study this carefully.

To Know the Times

"To know the times" means understanding the enemy's condition during battle. Is their energy rising or falling? By watching the mood of the enemy's troops and securing the best position, you can figure out their condition and move your forces accordingly. This principle of strategy lets you fight from a position of advantage. In a duel, you must anticipate the enemy and strike after learning their school of strategy, recognizing their strengths and weaknesses, and finding the right moment. Attack when they least expect it, knowing their timing and rhythm. Knowing the times means that if you're skilled enough, you can see through things clearly. If you're experienced in strategy, you'll recognize the enemy's plans and find many opportunities to win. You must study this thoroughly.

To Tread Down the Sword

"To tread down the sword" is a concept often used in strategy. First, in large-scale strategy, when the enemy starts by firing arrows or guns and then charges, it's hard to attack back if you're still busy reloading your own weapons. The idea is to attack swiftly while the enemy is still shooting. The spirit is to win by pressing forward while receiving the enemy's attack. In single combat, you can't secure a victory by following the enemy's sword swings with your own, going back and forth. You must beat them right at the start of their attack, stepping in forcefully so they can't continue. "Treading" doesn't just mean stepping on with your feet. It's about using your whole body, your spirit, and of course, your sword to step in and attack. You need to develop the mindset of not letting the enemy attack a second time. This is the spirit of taking control in every sense. Once you're in position, don't just aim to strike but follow through with your attack. You must study this deeply.

To Know Collapse

Everything can collapse—houses, bodies, and enemies—when their rhythm is thrown off. In large-scale strategy, when the enemy starts to collapse, you must chase them down and not let the chance slip away. If you don't take advantage of their collapse, they might recover. In single combat, the enemy might lose their timing and falter. If you don't act on this, they might regain their balance and become more cautious afterward. Focus on the enemy's collapse, pursue them, and attack without giving them a chance to recover. You must do this. Your pursuit should be forceful. You need to completely overpower the enemy so they can't regain their position. You must understand how to utterly defeat the enemy.

To Become the Enemy

"To become the enemy" means putting yourself in the enemy's position. People often see a robber trapped in a house as if they're a fortified enemy. But if you think of "becoming the enemy," you'll feel like the whole world is against you with no way out. The one trapped is the prey, while the one coming to capture is the predator. You must recognize this. In large-scale strategy, people often assume the enemy is stronger than they are, making them overly cautious. But if you have strong soldiers, know the principles of strategy, and understand how to defeat the enemy, there's nothing to fear. In single combat, you must also put yourself in the enemy's position. If you think, "Here is a master of the Way, someone who knows strategy," then you'll surely lose. You must consider this deeply.

To Release Four Hands

"To release four hands" is a technique used when both you and the enemy are fighting with equal determination, and neither side is winning. In this case, you need to let go of that mindset and win by using a different tactic. In large-scale strategy, when you find yourself in a "four hands" situation, don't give up—it's part of life. Instead, immediately change your approach and win by doing something the enemy doesn't expect. In single combat, if you feel stuck in a "four hands" situation, defeat the enemy by changing your mindset and using a technique that fits the situation. You must be able to judge when to do this.

To Move the Shade

"To move the shade" is used when you can't see the enemy's intentions. In large-scale strategy, when the enemy's position is unclear, act like you are about to launch a strong attack to force them to reveal their resources. Once you see what they have, it becomes easier to defeat them using another method. In single combat, if the enemy takes a defensive stance with their long sword, hiding their intentions, make a fake attack to draw them out. The enemy will show their sword, thinking they've seen your strategy, and then you can take advantage of what they reveal to secure a victory. Be careful not to miss the right moment. Study this thoroughly.

To Hold Down a Shadow

"Holding down a shadow" is used when you can sense the enemy's intent to attack. In large-scale strategy, when the enemy starts their attack, if you pretend to strongly suppress their technique, they might change their plan. At this point, change your own approach and defeat them by anticipating their next move with an empty, flexible mind. In single combat, when the enemy shows strong intent, you must block it with precise timing, and defeat them by catching them off guard with your timing. You must study this thoroughly.

To Pass On

Many things can be passed on, like sleepiness or yawning. Time itself can be passed on, too. In large-scale strategy, when the enemy becomes agitated and seems ready to rush, remain completely calm. This calmness will affect the enemy, causing them to relax. Once you see that this mood has spread to them, you can defeat them by launching a strong attack with an empty, flexible mind. In single combat, you can win by relaxing your body and spirit, and then, at the moment the enemy relaxes, attacking swiftly and forcefully, taking them by surprise. This is similar to the idea of "getting someone drunk." You can also infect the enemy with boredom, carelessness, or weakness. Study this well.

To Cause Loss of Balance

There are many ways to cause a loss of balance. Danger, hardship, or surprise can all lead to imbalance. You must study this closely. In large-scale strategy, it's important to unbalance the enemy. Attack suddenly where they don't expect it, and while their spirit is unsettled, keep pressing your advantage to defeat them. In single combat, start by moving slowly, then suddenly attack with full force. Don't give them any time to recover; keep the pressure on and seize the opportunity to win. Learn how to do this.

To Frighten

Fear often comes from the unexpected. In large-scale strategy, you can frighten the enemy not just by what they see, but by shouting, making a small force seem larger, or by surprising them with an unexpected attack from the side. All these things can create fear. You can win by taking advantage of the enemy's fearful state. In single combat, you should also take advantage of the enemy's surprise, using your body, sword, or voice to startle and defeat them. Study this well.

To Soak In

When you and the enemy are locked together, and you realize you can't make progress, "soak in" and become one with the enemy. You can win by using the right technique while you are intertwined. In both large and small battles, you can often achieve a decisive victory by learning how to "soak" into the enemy, while drawing apart might cause you to lose your chance to win. Study this carefully.

To Injure the Corners

It's hard to move strong things by pushing them directly, so you should "injure the corners." In large-scale strategy, it's helpful to strike at the edges of the enemy's forces. When the corners fall, the spirit of the entire group will fall apart. To defeat the enemy, you must follow up the attack once the corners have collapsed. In single combat, it becomes easy to win once the enemy's defenses break down. This happens when you injure the corners of his body, weakening him. It's important to know how to do this, so you must study it deeply.

To Throw into Confusion

This means making the enemy lose focus. In large-scale strategy, we can use our troops to throw the enemy into disarray on the battlefield. By observing the enemy's mood, we can make them think, "Here? There? Like this? Like that? Slow? Fast?" Victory is certain when the enemy gets caught up in a confusing rhythm that distracts their spirit. In single combat, we can confuse the enemy by using a variety of techniques when the moment is right. Fake a thrust or cut, or make the enemy think you're about to engage directly. Once the enemy is confused, it's easy to win. This is the core of fighting, and you must study it carefully.

The Three Shouts

The three shouts happen at different moments: before, during, and after. Shout based on the situation. The voice is a sign of life. We shout at fires, against the wind, and over waves. The voice shows energy. In large-scale strategy, we shout as loudly as possible at the beginning of battle. During the fight, the shout is low and fierce as we strike. After victory, we shout again to proclaim success. These are the three shouts. In single combat, we make a cut and shout "Ei!" at the same time to disturb the enemy, and after the shout, we strike with the long sword. We shout again after cutting down the enemy to announce victory. This is called "sen go no koe" (before and after voice). We do not shout at the same time we swing the sword. Instead, the shout helps establish rhythm. You must study this well.

To Mingle

In battle, when the armies face off, attack the enemy's strong points and, once you've pushed them back, quickly separate and strike another strong point on the edges of their forces. The spirit of this is like a winding mountain path. This is an important tactic when fighting one man against many. Defeat the enemies in one area or drive them back, then time your attack on other strong points to the right and left, moving like a winding path through the mountains, evaluating the enemy's strength. Once you understand the enemy's situation, attack fiercely without any hesitation. "Mingling" means advancing and engaging the enemy without stepping back. You must grasp this concept.

To Crush

This means crushing the enemy, viewing them as weak. In large-scale strategy, if the enemy has few men or even if they have many but their spirit is weak and confused, you must "knock the hat over their eyes," crushing them completely. If you only half-crush them, they might recover. You must learn the spirit of crushing as if with a firm grip. In single combat, if the enemy is less skilled, their rhythm is off, or they're retreating or evading, you should crush them immediately. Do this without giving them space to recover. The key is to crush them all at once. The main goal is to make sure they don't regain their position even a little. Study this deeply.

The Mountain-Sea Change

The "mountain-sea" spirit means that it's a mistake to repeat the same tactic multiple times when fighting the enemy. You may have to do something twice, but don't try it a third time. If you've attacked once and failed, there's little chance you'll succeed using the same approach again. If you try a technique again after it's failed twice, you must change your strategy. If the enemy expects you to act like the mountains, attack like the sea; if they expect you to act like the sea, attack like the mountains. You must study this deeply.

To Penetrate the Depths

When fighting the enemy, even if you can see you're winning on the surface by following the Way, the enemy's spirit might still be strong. They could be beaten on the outside but undefeated inside. With the principle of "penetrating the depths," you can crush the enemy's spirit by quickly shifting your own spirit. This happens often.

"Penetrating the depths" means using the long sword, your body, and your spirit to break through. This can't be explained in simple terms. Once you've crushed the enemy in the depths, you don't need to stay aggressive. But if the enemy's spirit remains strong, it's hard to defeat them. You must practice penetrating the depths in both large-scale strategy and single combat.

To Renew

"To renew" applies when you're fighting and the situation feels stuck, with no clear way forward. Abandon your current mindset, think of the situation with a fresh perspective, and win using a new rhythm. To renew, when you're deadlocked with the enemy, means that without changing your surroundings, you change your spirit and win using a different technique. You must also consider how "to renew" applies in large-scale strategy. Study this diligently.

Rat's Head, Ox's Neck

"Rat's head and ox's neck" means that when you and the enemy are both caught up in small, entangled details, you must always remember to think of the Way of Strategy as both small like a rat's head and large like an ox's neck. Whenever you get bogged down in small matters, switch to a large, open spirit, balancing the small with the large. This is one of the key ideas in strategy. A warrior must always think this way in everyday life. You should not stray from this idea in large-scale strategy or single combat.

The Commander Knows the Troops

"The commander knows the troops" applies everywhere in the Way of strategy. Using the wisdom of strategy, treat the enemy like they're your own troops. When you think this way, you can move them as you please and easily chase them around. You become the general, and the enemy becomes your soldiers. You must master this.

To Let Go the Hilt

There are many ways to "let go the hilt." One involves winning without even using a sword. Another is holding the long sword but not winning. These different methods can't be explained fully in writing. You must train well.

The Body of a Rock

When you've mastered the Way of Strategy, you can make your body like a rock, and nothing can touch you. This is the body of a rock. You will be unmoved. (Oral tradition)

Everything written above is what I have always thought about in Ichi school sword fighting, written down as it came to me. This is the first time I've written about my technique, so the order may seem a bit unclear. It's difficult to express it exactly. This book is a spiritual guide for anyone who wants to learn the Way. From my youth, my heart has been set on the Way of Strategy. I have trained my hand, strengthened my body, and developed many spiritual attitudes related to sword fighting.

If we look at men of other schools, they often focus on discussing theories and mastering hand techniques, and though they may seem skilled, they lack true spirit. Of course, men who train like this believe they are strengthening their body and spirit, but this is actually a barrier to the true Way, and its negative influence lingers forever. Because of this, the true Way of Strategy is declining and fading away. The true Way of sword fighting is the craft of defeating the enemy in battle, and nothing more. If you achieve and stick to the wisdom of my strategy, you will never doubt your victory.

Chapter 4 - The Wind Book

In strategy, you must understand the Ways of other schools, so I've written about different traditions of strategy in this Wind Book. Without knowing the Ways of other schools, it's hard to grasp the essence of my Ichi school. When we look at other schools, we find some that focus on using strength with extra-long swords. Some schools study the Way of the short sword, known as the kodachi. Others teach many sword techniques, describing sword positions as the "surface" and the Way as the "interior." I make it clear in this book that none of these are the true Way—along with all their faults, strengths, and rights and wrongs. My Ichi school is different. Other schools use their accomplishments as a way to make a living, like growing flowers and painting decorations to sell. But this is not the Way of Strategy. Some of the world's strategists only focus on sword-fighting and limit their training to handling the long sword and moving their bodies. But is skill alone enough to win? This isn't the essence of the Way. I have written down what's lacking in other schools, one by one, in this book. You must study these points closely to understand the value of my Ni To Ichi school.

Some other schools favor using extra-long swords. From the perspective of my strategy, these schools are weak. This is because they don't understand the idea of cutting the enemy by any means. They rely on the length of the extra-long sword, thinking they can defeat the enemy from a distance. In this world, it's said, "One inch gives the hand an advantage," but this is just idle talk from someone who doesn't know strategy. It shows a weak spirit to depend on the length of a sword, fighting from a distance without the benefit of true strategy. Perhaps this school likes extra-long swords as part of their teachings, but if we compare it to real life, it doesn't make sense. Should we necessarily lose if we have only a short sword and no long sword? It's hard for these people to cut the enemy up close because the long sword is too big and becomes a burden. It puts them at a disadvantage compared to someone with a short sword. As the saying goes: "Great and small go together." So, don't automatically dislike extra-long swords. What I dislike is the tendency to favor the long sword. In large-scale strategy, we can think of large forces as long swords and small forces as short swords. Can't a small group fight a large group? There are many examples of small forces defeating larger ones. Your strategy doesn't matter if you're called to fight in a small space but still wish for a long sword, or if you're in a house and only have your short sword. Besides, some people are not as strong as others. In my teaching, I dislike narrow-minded thinking. You must study this well.

You shouldn't talk about long swords being strong or weak. If you swing a long sword with only strength in mind, your cut will be rough, and it'll be harder to win. If you focus too much on the sword's strength, you'll try to cut too hard and end up not cutting well at all. It's also bad to test your sword by trying to cut too forcefully. Whenever you cross swords with an enemy, you shouldn't think about cutting them either too strongly or too weakly—just focus on cutting and killing them. Be focused entirely on killing the enemy. Don't try to cut too forcefully, and don't worry about cutting too softly either. Just focus on killing. If you rely on strength, when you hit the enemy's sword, you'll hit too hard, and your own sword will get carried away by the impact. That's why the saying "The strongest hand wins" doesn't hold true. In large-scale strategy, if you have a strong army and depend on strength to win, but the enemy also has a strong army, the fight will be fierce on both sides. Without the right principles, the battle can't be won. The spirit of my school is to win with the wisdom of strategy, ignoring unnecessary details. Study this well.

Using a shorter long sword is not the true Way to victory. In ancient times, tachi and katana referred to long and short swords. Men who are strong can handle even a long sword easily, so there's no reason for them to prefer the short sword. They also use long weapons like spears and halberds. Some people use a shorter long sword, thinking they can quickly stab the enemy when his guard is down as he swings his sword. But this way of thinking is wrong. Trying to take advantage of the enemy's unguarded moments is purely defensive and not a good strategy for close combat. Plus, if you face many enemies, you can't use the tactic of jumping in with a short sword. Some believe that if they face a group of enemies with a shorter long sword, they can move freely, cutting wide arcs, but in reality, they'll have to constantly defend themselves and eventually get caught up with the enemy. This approach doesn't align with the true Way of Strategy. The sure way to win is to confuse the enemy by making him move aside, all while keeping your body firm and upright. The same principle applies in large-scale strategy. The essence of strategy is to fall upon the enemy in large numbers and quickly defeat them. People who study strategy tend to get used to countering, dodging, and retreating as normal tactics. They become stuck in this habit and can easily be led around by the enemy. The Way of Strategy is straightforward and direct. You must chase the enemy, making him follow your will.

Other Schools with Many Methods of Using the Long Sword

Placing too much importance on the positions of the long sword is a flawed way of thinking. What is called "attitude" in the world refers to when there is no enemy. This has been the tradition since ancient times, and there should be no idea of "this is the modern way" in dueling. You must put the enemy in uncomfortable positions. Attitude is for times when you must hold your ground, like defending castles, setting up battle formations, and showing that you won't be moved, even by a strong attack. In the Way of dueling, however, you should always focus on taking the lead and attacking. Attitude is about waiting for an attack. You must understand this. In duels of strategy, you should shift the enemy's attitude. Attack where his spirit is weak, confuse him, make him anxious, and frighten him. Use the enemy's unsettled rhythm to your advantage, and you will win. I do not like the defensive spirit known as "attitude." Therefore, in my Way, there is something called "Attitude-No Attitude."

In large-scale strategy, we position our troops for battle by considering our own strength, observing the enemy's numbers, and noting the battlefield's details. This is at the start of the battle. The spirit of attacking first is entirely different from the spirit of being attacked. Withstanding an attack with a strong attitude and defending well is like building a wall of spears and halberds. When you attack the enemy, your spirit must be as strong as pulling the stakes out of the wall and using them as spears and halberds. You must study this closely.

Fixing the Eyes in Other Schools

Some schools teach that you should fix your eyes on the enemy's long sword. Others say you should watch their hands, their face, or their feet, and so on. But if you focus on these spots, your spirit can get confused, and your strategy will fall apart. Let me explain this in detail. Soccer players don't fix their eyes on the ball, but by playing well on the field, they perform skillfully. When you are used to something, your eyes don't limit you. People like master musicians have the music right in front of them, or swordsmen move their blades in different ways when they have mastered the Way. But this doesn't mean they stare directly at these things or make useless movements. It means they can see naturally.

In the Way of Strategy, after you have fought many battles, you will naturally assess the speed and position of the enemy's sword. Once you've mastered the Way, you will also see the strength of their spirit. In strategy, "fixing the eyes" means gazing at the enemy's heart. In large-scale strategy, you should focus on the enemy's strength. "Perception" and "sight" are the two ways of seeing. Perception involves focusing intensely on the enemy's spirit, watching the condition of the battlefield, keeping your gaze steady, noticing the flow of the battle, and observing the changes in advantage. This is the way to win. In single combat, don't focus on small details. As I've said, if you focus on details and ignore what really matters, your spirit will get confused, and victory will slip away. Study this principle carefully and train hard.

Use of the Feet in Other Schools

There are different ways of using the feet: floating foot, jumping foot, springing foot, treading foot, crow's foot, and other nimble walking methods. From the viewpoint of my strategy, all of these are unsatisfactory. I dislike floating foot because the feet tend to float during a fight. The Way must be grounded. I also don't like jumping foot because it leads to a habit of jumping and a restless spirit. No matter how much you jump, it doesn't have a real purpose, so jumping is bad. Springing foot causes a springy, uncertain spirit. Treading foot is a "waiting" method, and I especially dislike it. Besides these, there are various fast walking methods, like crow's foot, and others.

Sometimes, however, you may face the enemy on difficult terrain like marshland, swampy ground, river valleys, rocky areas, or narrow roads. In these situations, you can't jump or move your feet quickly. In my strategy, the footwork remains the same. I walk as I normally do on the street. You should never lose control of your feet. Based on the enemy's rhythm, move either fast or slow, adjusting your body just enough—not too much or too little. Moving your feet properly is also crucial in large-scale strategy. If you attack quickly and carelessly without understanding the enemy's spirit, your rhythm will be thrown off, and you won't be able to win. On the other hand, if you advance too slowly, you won't be able to take advantage of the enemy's disorder, and the chance to win will pass. The battle will drag on, and you won't finish it quickly. You must win by seizing on the enemy's confusion and not giving them even the slightest chance to recover. Practice this thoroughly.

Speed in Other Schools

Speed is not part of the true Way of Strategy. Speed can make things seem fast or slow depending on whether or not they follow the right rhythm. In any Way, a true master of strategy doesn't seem fast. Some people can walk a hundred or even a hundred and twenty miles in a day, but this doesn't mean they run all day long. Untrained runners might seem like they've been running the entire time, but their performance is poor. In dance, skilled performers can sing while dancing, but beginners slow down and become overwhelmed. Similarly, the "old pine tree" melody played on a drum is calm, but beginners make it sound rushed and busy. Very skilled people can handle a fast rhythm, but rushing is bad. If you try to go too fast, you'll fall out of time. Of course, going too slow is also bad. Truly skilled people never lose their timing, and they are always deliberate without seeming busy. This principle can be understood from these examples. What is known as "speed" is especially harmful in the Way of Strategy. The reason is that in different places—like marshes or swamps—you may not be able to move your body and legs quickly together. And it's even harder to cut quickly with a long sword in these situations. If you try to cut fast, as if you're using a fan or a short sword, you won't make an effective cut at all. You must understand this.

In large-scale strategy, a fast, frantic spirit is also undesirable. Your spirit should be calm, like holding down a pillow, so you won't be even a little late. When your opponent is rushing recklessly, you must act the opposite way—stay calm and steady. Don't let yourself be affected by the opponent's pace. Train diligently to master this spirit.

"Interior" and "Surface" in Other Schools

There is no "interior" or "surface" in strategy. In the arts, people often claim to have hidden meanings, secret traditions, and talk about "interior" and "gate," but in combat, there is no such thing as fighting on the surface or cutting with the interior. When I teach my Way, I start by showing techniques that are easy for students to understand, a straightforward teaching. Gradually, I explain deeper principles, things that are hard to grasp, depending on the student's progress. In any case, because true understanding comes through experience, I don't talk about "interior" or "gate."

In life, if you go deep into the mountains, even deeper, you will eventually reach the gate. Whatever the Way, it has an interior, and sometimes it's useful to point out the gate. In strategy, however, we cannot clearly say what is hidden and what is revealed. That's why I don't like passing on my Way through written pledges or rules. By observing my students' abilities, I teach the direct Way, removing the bad influence of other schools, and gradually introduce them to the true Way of the warrior. The way I teach strategy is through a trustworthy spirit. You must train diligently.

I've tried to outline the strategy of other schools in the nine sections above. I could now go into detail about these schools one by one, from the "gate" to the "interior," but I've intentionally not named the schools or their key points. The reason is that different branches of schools interpret the teachings in various ways. As opinions differ, so must interpretations of the same idea. Therefore, no single person's understanding applies to any school. I've shown the general tendencies of other schools across nine points. If we look at them honestly, we see that people tend to favor either long swords or short swords and focus too much on strength in both large and small matters. This explains why I don't deal with the "gates" of other schools.

In my Ichi school of the long sword, there is no gate or interior. There is no hidden meaning in sword positions. You simply need to keep your spirit true to fully realize the virtue of strategy.

Chapter 5 - The Book Of The Void

The Ni To Ichi Way of Strategy is written down in this Book of the Void. The spirit of the void is what we call a place where nothing exists. It's something beyond human knowledge. The void is, of course, nothingness. By understanding things that exist, you can also understand what does not exist—that is the void. People in this world often misunderstand and believe that whatever they don't understand must be the void. But this isn't the true void; it's confusion. In the Way of Strategy, some warriors believe that anything they don't comprehend in their craft must be the void. This, too, is not the true void.

To truly master the Way of Strategy as a warrior, you must fully study all martial arts and never stray from the Way of the warrior. With a calm spirit, practice every day and every hour. Strengthen both your spirit and mind, and refine both your perception and your sight. When your spirit is completely clear, without even a hint of confusion, that is when you reach the true void. Until you find the true Way—whether in Buddhism or in everyday life—you might think everything is correct and orderly. But when we look at things objectively, through the laws of the world, we see many ideas that have strayed from the true Way.

Understand this well, and let straightforwardness be your foundation, with the true spirit as your Way. Practice strategy broadly, correctly, and openly. Then, you will begin to see things from a wider perspective, and by taking the void as your Way, you will see the Way as the void. In the void, there is virtue and no evil. Wisdom exists, principles exist, the Way exists, but the spirit is nothingness.

Twelfth day of the fifth month,

Second year of Shoho (1645).

Teruro Magonojo

SHINMEN MUSASHI

The Tao Te Ching

Laozi

Shang Pian

Chapter 1

The Dao that can be spoken is not the eternal Dao;
The name that can be named is not the eternal name.
The nameless is the source of heaven and earth;
The named is the mother of all things.
Therefore,
Without desire, you see the mystery's beginning;
With desire, you see its manifestations.
Though they come from the same source, they are different in
  name;
Both are called the Mystery.
Mystery within Mystery, the gateway to all wonders.

Chapter 2

Everyone understands what beauty is;
That is because there is ugliness.
Everyone knows what goodness is;
That is because there is evil.
Therefore,
Being and nothingness give birth to one another,
Hard and easy create each other,
Long and short define each other,
High and low complete each other,
Music and sound harmonize with each other,
Front and back follow one another.
Thus,
The sage focuses on non-action in his works,
Practices silence in his words.
The myriad things arise but are left alone,
The sage creates but does not possess,
Acts but does not claim,

Achieves but does not take credit.
Because he does not seek credit, it never leaves him.

Chapter 3

Not seeking virtue
keeps the people from competing.
Not valuing rare treasures
keeps the people from becoming thieves.
Not displaying what is desirable
keeps the people's hearts undisturbed.
Therefore, in the sage's peaceful and quiet world,
People's minds are calm,
Their bellies are full,
Their ambitions are reduced,
Their bodies are strong.
People are kept unknowing and without desire,
And even those who know do not dare to act.
Acting without action,
Nothing is left undone.

Chapter 4

The Dao is empty,
Not seeking virtue
keeps the people from competing.
Not valuing rare treasures
keeps the people from becoming thieves.
Not displaying what is desirable
keeps the people's hearts undisturbed.
Therefore, in the sage's peaceful and quiet world,
People's minds are calm,
Their bellies are full,
Their ambitions are reduced,
Their bodies are strong.
People are kept unknowing and without desire,

And even those who know do not dare to act.
Acting without action,
Nothing is left undone.

Chapter 5

The sky and the earth do not show kindness,
They treat the myriad things like straw dogs.
The sage does not show kindness,
He treats people like straw dogs.
The space between heaven and earth, how like a great bellows!
Empty, yet never exhausted,
Move it, and wind comes forth.
Too many words lead to nothing.
It is better to stay balanced between extremes.

Chapter 6

The valley-spirit never dies; it is called the primal mother.
The gate of the primal mother is the root of the world.
Her supply is endless,
Using her will never deplete her.

Chapter 7

Heaven and earth are eternal.
The reason heaven and earth endure
Is because they do not live for themselves,
Therefore, they last forever.
Because of this, the sage places himself behind others,
Yet finds himself ahead.
He is unconcerned with discomfort and danger,
Yet he survives.
Is it not because he is selfless
That he ultimately achieves fulfillment?

Chapter 8

The best character is like water.
Water's virtue is that it benefits all things without competing,
And it flows to places that others avoid,
Thus, it is close to the Dao.
It is good to live on solid ground,
To deepen the heart,
To love people when among them,
To keep one's word when speaking,
To be at peace when governing,
To do what one is capable of,
To act at the right moment.
Because it does not compete,
It is without blame.

Chapter 9

Rather than filling a cup until it overflows, it is better to stop in
    time.
Hammering and sharpening will soon wear it down.
Filling a hall with riches, one cannot protect it.
The man who is arrogant from great wealth invites disaster.
Stepping back after success aligns with the way of the universe.

Chapter 10

If the soul keeps being controlled by the body,
How can the body and soul not separate?
Forcing oneself to appear delicate,
How can one remain like a baby?
Clean the mirror of the true source,
How can it not reveal its flaws?
To love people and govern a country,
How can one not appoint the wise?
The gate of heaven opens and closes constantly,
How can one act like a passive observer?

Having understood causes and effects,
How can one stick to unfinished tasks?
Nurture and nourish them,
Create without possessing,
Act without claiming,
Lead without controlling.
This is called profound virtue.

Chapter 11

Join thirty spokes to a single hub,
It is the empty space at the center that makes the wheel useful.
Shape clay into a vessel,
It is the empty space inside that makes the vessel useful.
Cut doors and windows for a room,
It is the empty space within that makes the room useful.
Thus, what is made provides only the form,
But what we use is the original empty space.

Chapter 12

Beautiful colors blind people's eyes,
Appealing music deafens people's ears,
Delicious flavors dull people's taste,
Indulging in hunting drives people's hearts wild,
Pursuing rare treasures leads to improper behavior.
Thus, the sage focuses on the inner world, not the outer.
He discards the outer and embraces the inner.

Chapter 13

Honor and disgrace are equally alarming,
And great troubles arise because of the body.
What does it mean by "Honor and disgrace are equally alarming"?
Honor is fleeting,
It is frightening to receive it, and frightening to lose it.

This is what is meant by "Honor and disgrace are equally alarming."
What does it mean by "Great trouble is like the body"?
The reason I have great trouble is because I have a body;
If I had no body, what trouble could I have?
Therefore, if you view your body as the world,
you can be trusted to govern the world;
If you cherish your body as the world,
you are worthy of caring for the world.

Chapter 14

That which can be seen but not observed is called invisible;
That which can be heard but not perceived is called soundless;
That which can be touched but not grasped is called intangible.
These three cannot be fully understood, and so they merge into one.
Above, it is not bright; below, it is not dark.
A continuous thread without a name returns to the formless.
It is called the form of the formless, the image of the imageless.
This is called the indistinct and mysterious.
Approach it, and you cannot see its front; follow it, and you cannot see its back.
By holding onto the Dao of the present, you can master the present moment and understand the origins of the past.
This is called the thread of the Dao.

Chapter 15

Once upon a time, those who knew the Way were mysterious and subtle people,
Fleeting yet deep, tranquil yet utterly unfathomable.
Since they are difficult to describe, I can only speak of what they seemed like:
Cautious, as if crossing a winter river,
Wary, as if fearful of their neighbors.

Solemn, like courteous house guests.

Elusive, like melting ice.

Pure and natural, like uncut gems.

Vast and open, like a deep valley.

Yet mysterious, oh yes, like troubled waters.

Who can stay calm amidst the turbulence, allowing clarity to emerge from within?

Who can remain at peace eternally, allowing movement to give birth to nature?

For those who follow the Way, fulfillment was never their goal.

Only because they are never fully satisfied, they can continuously find renewal.

Chapter 16

Immersed in the heart of the void, hold on to the essence of tranquility.

The myriad things arise together,

And through this, I see their returning.

Now things bloom, and in blooming, each one returns to its source.

Returning to the source is called tranquility,

This is the return to destiny,

The return to destiny is eternal,

To know the eternal is wisdom.

Not knowing wisdom leads to disaster!

Knowing the eternal brings vast understanding,

Vast understanding leads to open-mindedness,

Open-mindedness leads to being regal,

Being regal leads to being heavenly,

Being heavenly leads to the Dao,

The Dao leads to everlasting.

Thus, one can face the perishing of the body without fear.

Chapter 17

Great rulers are barely known by their subjects,
Next come those the people draw near and praise,
Then those the people fear,
And finally, those the people despise.
If a ruler lacks trust, trust will not be given.
Act without arrogance;
Achieve without boasting;
When deeds are done, the people will say it happened naturally.

Chapter 18

When the Dao is lost, benevolence and righteousness arise.
When prudence and wisdom emerge, hypocrisy grows.
When family relationships are in disorder, filial piety and parental affection appear.
When the state is in chaos, loyalty and faithfulness are proclaimed.

Chapter 19

Abandon holiness, relinquish wisdom; the people will thrive a hundredfold.
Abandon benevolence, relinquish righteousness; the people will return to filial piety and affection.
Abandon cleverness, relinquish profit; and thieves and robbers will disappear.
As I know these three are not just empty words,
Hold fast to what is trustworthy.
Embrace simplicity, cherish purity,
Lessen the self, and diminish desires.

Chapter 20

Discard conventional doctrines, and be free from anxieties.
Flattery or reprimand, what difference does it make?
Good or evil, what does it matter?
Just because people are in awe, must you remain indifferent?

Ridiculous! Baseless!
When everyone is celebrating with joy,
As if they've achieved a spiritual victory,
As if they're enjoying a great feast,
I alone am empty, contemplating the endless future,
Dazed like a newborn,
Living in the moment, pondering the unknown.
When everyone feels full,
I alone feel hollow.
I am a fool! Confused!
When everyone seems enlightened, I alone am in doubt;
When everyone is alert, I alone am lost.
Mysterious! Like the dim twilight,
Vast! Like the infinite universe.
When everyone is focused, I alone am stubborn and lowly.
I alone am different from the ordinary,
I find refuge in the embrace of this profound Dao.

Chapter 21

Where the greatest Virtue resides,
Only the Dao can reveal it.
Things that embody the Dao
Shine with freedom and ease.
Eased! Liberated from form, yet perfectly shaped;
Freed! At ease with its place, yet steady.
Mesmerizing! Mysterious!
A light shines from within;
Its radiance so pure, it reveals the truth.
Through all time,
Its name remains undiminished,
Gathering all the marvels of human understanding.
How do I know the essence of all these wonders?
By observing things that embody the Dao.

Chapter 22

Fractured, one seeks unity,
Crooked, one strives for straightness,
Depressed, one appears fulfilled,
Exhausted, one shows freshness,
Ignorant, one expresses wisdom,
Excessive, one becomes misguided.
Thus, the master upholds integrity,
And sets an example for the people.
Without professing, enlightenment is revealed,
Without contending, brilliance shines,
Without proclaiming, praises are won,
Without demanding dignity, respect is earned.
The master does not compete,
Therefore remains uncontested.
"Fractured, one seeks unity"—
Such timeless wisdom!
With true integrity, one rediscovers oneself.

Chapter 23

Speak less, and words will naturally express themselves.
Thus, gusts cannot chill a vibrant day,
Showers cannot turn daylight into dusk.
Why is this so?
Even heaven and earth cannot resist their own force,
How can people do so?
Therefore, those who follow the Dao find joy in knowing that:
The Dao is the teaching,
Virtue is the Virtue,
And perplexity is simply perplexity.
Aligned with the Dao, the Dao welcomes them;
Aligned with Virtue, Virtue appreciates them;
Aligned with perplexity, even perplexity satisfies them.
A lack of faith

Explains why disbelief persists in this seeming futility.

Chapter 24

Those who tip-toe cannot stand firm,
Those who stride cannot walk steadily,
Those who show off do not shine,
Those who are self-righteous lack true justification.
Those who assert themselves achieve nothing,
Those who esteem themselves do not endure.
According to the Dao,
These are called excess and arrogance,
Which the people despise.
Therefore, those who embrace the Dao do not dwell in such ways.

Chapter 25

Before existence,
Before the birth of heaven and earth,
It was tranquil, desolate!
Independent and unmoved,
Cyclic and unbroken,
The mother of all nature.
Its true name is unknown,
I call it the Art of the Dao,
And describe it as great.
Being great, it is far-reaching,
Being far-reaching, it is distant,
Being distant, it returns.
Thus, the Dao is great,
Heaven is great,
Earth is great,
And the master is also great.
These are the four noble greatnesses,
And the master is one of them.
Humanity follows the earth,

The earth follows heaven,
Heaven follows the Dao,
The Dao follows nature.

Chapter 26

Heaviness is the root of lightness,
Temperance is the master of temperament.
Therefore, the master stays close to essential resources in their
    endeavors;
Even when there are sights and distractions,
They remain calm and composed.
Why then would a leader of many followers,
Risk their own body in pursuit of the world?
Being light, they lose their root;
Being tempestuous, they forfeit mastery.

Chapter 27

Good traveling leaves no tracks;
Good speech leaves no room for reproach;
Good strategies require no scheming;
Good fastening needs no hinges, yet no door can be opened;
The good knot is tied without a rope, and it cannot be undone.
Thus, the Sage never fails to save people,
Therefore, no one is rejected;
The Sage never fails to save things,
Therefore, nothing is abandoned.
This is true illumination.
Thus, the good are teachers to the bad,
And the bad are resources for the good.
One who fails to respect their teacher,
And does not cherish their resources,
No matter how intelligent, is deeply confused.
This is the essential mystery!

Chapter 28

Gain knowledge of the external, but
Acquaint yourself with the internal, and
Become the wellspring of the earth.
Be the earth's fountain, be Virtuous and unwavering,
And be renewed.
Recognize the brilliance of the spotlight, but
Stay in the shadows, and
Become an example for the people.
Be the people's example, be Virtuous without excess,
And find peace.
Know the glory, but
Show humility, and
Become the world's refuge.
Be the world's refuge, be Virtuous and content,
And return to your roots.
When uprooted, wood can be shaped into tools;
The master uses it to become a respected leader.
Thus, a great tailor seldom trims.

Chapter 29

It is futile to try to possess the universe,
Or to shape it according to one's ambitions.
The workings of the universe cannot be controlled,
One cannot act upon them.
Act upon them, and you will fail;
Grasp them, and they will slip away.
For everything, there is a time to advance and a time to retreat,
A time to blow and a time to breathe,
A time for strength and a time for weakness,
A time to carry and a time to ride.
Thus, the master avoids extremes,
Avoids extravagance, and avoids grandeur.

Chapter 30

Those who offer advice on the Art of governance
Do not recommend using force to dominate the world,
Understanding it invites retaliation.
Where troops march, thorns grow.
After great armies, years of resentment follow.
Thus, the master aims only to achieve the goal,
Daring not to seek dominance.
Accomplish, but avoid glorification,
Accomplish, but restrain aggression,
Accomplish, but reject pride,
Accomplish only because it is necessary,
Accomplish, but refuse domination.
Things that mature grow old,
This is not the Way of the Dao.
Without following the Dao, one perishes prematurely.

Chapter 31

Where everyone is heavily armed, the state is in vain,
Such actions are resented,
Therefore, the master does not dwell there.
Thus, the master finds refuge in what remains,
And acts based on righteousness.
Weapons are tools of destruction,
They are not the instruments of a master.
Used only when absolutely necessary,
Peace and reconciliation are paramount,
Victory is achieved without glorification.
Those who glorify victory take pleasure in bloodshed,
And those who take pleasure in bloodshed
Cannot win the hearts of the people.
Therefore, in times of prosperity, remain humble,
In adversity, act with righteousness.
Thus, the general stands on the left,

The admiral stands on the right,
In solemn remembrance.
Casualties are mourned with consolation,
And victories are remembered with solemnity.

Chapter 32

The Dao remains eternally unknowable.
Its unexploited nature may seem insignificant,
Yet no one under heaven can control it.
When kings and nobles abide by it,
The myriad things naturally follow.
Heaven and earth work together,
To bring about the morning dew,
Without human intervention, the droplets spread evenly.
In society, establishments come with titles;
Once titles are given, one must learn restraint.
With self-restraint, disaster can be avoided.
In this way, the Dao manifests in the world,
Like rivers merging into the vast oceans.

Chapter 33

Knowing others is intelligence,
Knowing oneself is enlightenment.
Conquering others is strength,
Conquering oneself is true invincibility.
Those who are content are truly wealthy,
Those who are driven by ambition are enslaved by it.
Those who hold to their principles will endure,
Those who pass but are not forgotten live on.

Chapter 34

The implications of the Tao are vast and far-reaching. Ubiquitous!
It can influence and sway everything, to the left or right.
The myriad things depend on it, yet it never turns away,

Fulfilling all without seeking recognition.
It supports the myriad things without claiming ownership,
Always without desire,
Thus, it is called modest.
It is immersed in all things without taking possession,
Thus, it is called great.
Therefore, the master avoids seeking greatness,
And is thereby able to accomplish great deeds.

Chapter 35

Herald a great symbol,
And the people will come.
Come toward teachings that do no harm,
And the people will find safety,
Peace, and prosperity.
Music and temptations make the visitor linger.
The words of the Dao
Are tasteless and without sensation.
Look, and it cannot be seen,
Listen, and it cannot be heard,
Use it, and it cannot be exhausted.

Chapter 36

If one wishes to shrink something, one must first expand it greatly;
If one wishes to weaken something, one must first strengthen it
    greatly;
If one wishes to discard something, one must first allow it to
    flourish greatly;
If one wishes to obtain something, one must first give it
    abundantly.
This is the Knowledge of Subtlety.
Gentleness overcomes hardness,
Vulnerability overcomes dominance.
Fish cannot leave the depths,

Deadly weapons should not be shown to the people.

Chapter 37

The Dao remains in non-action, yet nothing is left undone.
When leaders follow this way,
The myriad things transform naturally.
When transformed, desires arise,
I would quiet them with the unexploited and unknowable.
Without knowledge or exploitation, one is led to no desire.
Without desire and in tranquility,
The world corrects itself.

Xia Pian

Chapter 38

Those with great Virtue are not confined by virtues,
Thus, they remain with Virtue.
Those without Virtue cannot free themselves from the rules of
    virtue,
Thus, they remain without Virtue.
Those with great Virtue act without seeking credit,
Those without Virtue act and demand recognition.
The humane act charitably without seeking reputation.
The righteous act in the name of justice and seek glory.
The moral act, but when there is no response,
They force the issue, alas, to no avail.
Thus, when the Dao is lost, there is Virtue;
When Virtue is lost, there is humanity;
When humanity is lost, there is righteousness;
When righteousness is lost, there is morality.
When the rituals of morality become customary,
Devotion and faith grow shallow, and turmoil begins to stir.
When scholars are given priority,
The Dao becomes glorified and used to deceive the masses.

Therefore, the master is concerned with depth,
Not with appearances;
Focuses on integrity, not on glory.
Thus, let go of the exterior and embrace the interior.

Chapter 39

When aligned with the Dao:
When heaven is at one, it is clear,
When earth is at one, it is fertile,
When the spirit is at one, it is calm,
When shelter is at one, it is secure,
When the myriad things are at one, there is life,
When leaders are at one, the people are respectful,
And all things become united.
If heaven loses its clarity, there is fear of collapse;
If earth becomes barren, there is dread of disaster;
If the spirit is disturbed, there is anxiety over death;
If shelter is deprived, there is panic over decline;
If the myriad things are lifeless, there is fear of extinction;
If leaders become disrespectful,
Obsessed with admiration for their own power,
The people grow terrified under authority.
Thus, true admiration stems from humility,
Supremacy finds its foundation in lowliness.
When leaders remain uninvolved, detached, and undeserving,
Is it not rooted in humility?
Therefore, prepare your chariots and set them aside.
Desire not crowns and jewels,
But remain composed in the grit and gravel.

Chapter 40

Resilience reflects the Dao in action,
Vulnerability shows the Dao in expression.
The myriad things in the universe are born from existence,

And existence is born from non-existence.

Chapter 41

The learned discover the Dao and follow it naturally;
The seeker discovers the Dao and questions its power;
The unlearned discover the Dao and burst into laughter,
Without their laughter, it wouldn't be the Dao.
Thus, the words of wisdom say:
Those enlightened by the Dao appear confused,
Those moving toward the Dao seem to fall behind,
Those who discredit the Dao seem honorable,
The Virtuous seem empty and desolate,
The honest seem humiliated,
Those with noble Virtue seem to lack,
Those who build on Virtue seem deceitful,
Those with principled character seem uncertain.
Great squareness has no sharp corners,
Great tools take time to craft,
Great vocalists rarely raise their voices,
Great symbols are formless.
The Dao is the master of providing and empowering.

Chapter 42

The Dao gives birth to unity,
Unity gives birth to duality,
Duality gives birth to trinity,
Trinity gives birth to the myriad things.
The myriad things carry shadows and embrace radiance,
Infused with the breath of life to achieve the harmony of darkness,
    light, and soul.
(People dislike being uninvolved, irrelevant, and undeserving,
Yet true leaders align themselves with these qualities.)
Thus, things may be gained by losing,
And may be lost by gaining.

What others proclaim, I will also declare:
"Forcing principles will not make them sustainable."
Let this be the heart and soul of the message.

Chapter 43

The softest in the world
Overcomes the hardest in the world.
What has no substance enters where there is no space.
Thus, we come to appreciate the benefits of non-action.
The teachings of unspoken words,
The power of inaction,
Few things in this world can compare.

Chapter 44

Fame and honor, which is more relatable?
Health and wealth, which is more essential?
Success and failure, which is more damaging?
Thus, great admiration comes with a heavy cost,
Accumulating treasures leads to the loss of modesty.
Embrace humility to avoid humiliation,
Know your limits to become limitless and enduring.

Chapter 45

Great support appears insufficient,
Yet when used, it does not fail.
Great buoyancy seems hollow,
Yet when utilized, it never runs out.
Great honesty appears flawed,
Great skill seems inept,
Great speech seems inarticulate.
Movement overcomes cold,
Stillness overcomes heat,
Through tranquility, the world finds its righteousness.

Chapter 46

When the world follows the Dao,
Carriages are used to transport manure.
When the world strays from the Dao,
Armed chariots line the city gates.
There is no greater sin than temptation,
No greater fault than discontent,
No greater guilt than constant desire.
Therefore, know contentment, and you will always have enough.

Chapter 47

Without leaving home,
You can understand the universe.
Without looking through windows of knowledge,
You can grasp the Dao.
The farther you travel, the less you may know.
Thus, the master does not travel, yet is wise,
Does not see, yet is insightful,
Does not act, yet is accomplished.

Chapter 48

In pursuing scholarship, each day brings something to gain.
In practicing the Dao, each day brings something to lose.
When you have lost all that can be lost,
You arrive at a state of non-action.
Act without acting, and nothing will be left undone!
Thus, those who can master the universe
Often remain unoccupied;
Those who are preoccupied
Cannot master the universe.

Chapter 49

The masters never close their minds,
But align their minds with the minds of the people.

To those who are kind, be kind;
To those who are unkind, be kind as well.
Kindness is the way of Virtue.
To those who are faithful, have faith in them;
To those who are unfaithful, have faith in them as well.
Faithfulness is the way of Virtue.
The master remains ever watchful over the world,
And is concerned for the people.
The people pay attention to the master's words and actions,
And the master nurtures them all in innocence.

Chapter 50

Emerging from birth and disappearing into death:
Three out of ten are followers of life,
Three out of ten are followers of death,
And three out of ten pursue life,
But end up in the place of death.
Why is this so?
Because they overindulge in their pursuit of life.
Those who truly understand the essence of living
Can walk through the forest without being attacked by tigers,
Enter battlefields without being harmed by weapons.
Brutality finds no way to strike,
Tigers find no place to lay their claws,
Enemies find no opening to lodge their swords.
Why is this so?
Because they never enter a realm of death.

Chapter 51

The Dao conceives,
Virtue nurtures,
Things take form,
Movement gives them power.
Thus, among the myriad things,

None fail to respect the Dao and honor Virtue.
Respect for the Dao,
Honor for Virtue,
Are not commanded, yet arise naturally.
Therefore, the Dao conceives, and Virtue nurtures,
Guides and educates,
Empowers and matures,
Raises and redeems.
Conceiving without possessing,
Acting without dwelling,
Leading without dictating—
These are the subtleties of Virtue.

Chapter 52

The origin of existence began with the mother of all nature.
Understand the mother,
And you will know the being of the child;
Understand the being of the child,
And you will reconnect with the mother.
One can face the perishing of the body without fear.
Close the exchanges,
Shut the doors,
And you will live without burdens.
Open the exchanges,
Engage in business,
And you will live without peace.
Seeing small details is to have insight,
Holding to gentleness is to have strength.
Use the radiance,
But return to your insight.
Remember, striving to leave nothing behind will leave yourself
    empty.
This is the practice of timeless truth.

Chapter 53

What makes one principled is having knowledge,
Walking the path of the Dao,
The only fear is becoming too instructive.
The way of the Dao is unmarked,
Yet people prefer having a clear path.
When many are appointed to offices, while fields grow wild,
And storages remain empty,
When fashion is overly adorned,
And people carry weapons,
When they indulge in feasts,
And revel in extravagance,
This is behaving like thieves!
It is not the way of the Dao.

Chapter 54

Proficient builders do not destroy,
Noble embracers do not abandon.
They remain honored through generations.
Cultivate the Dao within yourself,
And the Virtue lies in understanding the truth.
Cultivate the Dao within your family,
And the Virtue lies in finding fortune.
Cultivate the Dao within your community,
And the Virtue lies in earning respect.
Cultivate the Dao within your nation,
And the Virtue lies in reaping prosperity.
Cultivate the Dao within the universe,
And the Virtue is universally enjoyed.
Therefore, observe yourself to know yourself,
Observe your family to know your family,
Observe your community to know your community,
Observe your nation to know your nationality,
Observe the universe to know the universe.

How do I know the essence of the universe?
By observing all of this.

Chapter 55

The profoundness of being embraced by Virtue
Is like being a newborn.
Wild wasps, poisonous scorpions, and venomous snakes find no
    sting,
Fierce beasts find no grip,
Predatory birds find no claws.
The bones are weak, the muscles tender, yet the grasp is strong.
Without knowing the union of male and female,
Yet wholly united with integrity, embodying true purity.
Crying all day, yet the voice is not strained,
The very sound of harmony.
Understanding harmony leads to eternity,
Understanding eternity brings enlightenment.
Nurturing life is an act of grace,
Channeling energy inward is true strength.
Things that mature grow old,
Because they go against the Dao.
To go against the Dao
Is to meet an early end.

Chapter 56

Those who know do not speak,
Those who speak do not know.
Block its exchanges,
Constrain its ideas,
Temper its cleverness,
Unravel its complexity,
Soften its intensity,
And merge into its boundless nature.
This is the subtlety of the all-encompassing.

It cannot be possessed for love,
Cannot be possessed for hate,
Cannot be possessed for gain,
Cannot be possessed for harm,
Cannot be possessed for respect,
Cannot be possessed for contempt.
Thus, it is honored by the universe.

Chapter 57

Be just in governance,
Be unpredictable in battle,
Be unoccupied to master the universe.
How do I understand the essence of leadership?
With this:
When the world is full of taboos and prohibitions,
The people are steeped in poverty.
When the people are armed with weapons,
The nation is riddled with corruption.
When the people are consumed by professions,
Strange obsessions arise.
When laws and regulations multiply,
Thievery becomes common.
Therefore, the master maintains:
"I act not, and the people naturally flourish.
I believe in peace, and the people naturally become righteous.
I remain unoccupied, and the people naturally prosper.
I desire nothing, and the people naturally become serene."

Chapter 58

When governance is idle,
The people are calm and mellow;
When governance is strict,
The people become mischievous.
Adversity! Where fortune may lean,

Fortune! Where adversity hides.

How can the ultimate be known?

It has no fixed pattern!

As righteousness regresses into confusion,

Goodwill regresses into deception,

And the days become long and difficult.

Thus, the master remains square without being sharp,

Upright without being severe,

Straightforward without being thoughtless,

Radiant without seeking glory.

Chapter 59

In governance and management, nothing compares to being conservative.

Only by being conservative,

Can withdrawal lead to advancement.

Advancing through withdrawal means focusing on cultivating Virtue.

Focusing on Virtue,

Nothing becomes insurmountable.

When nothing is insurmountable, limitations become unknown.

When one's limitations are unknown,

One can inspire a nation.

A nation inspired is a nation that thrives.

This is being deeply rooted

In the viability and vision of the Dao.

Chapter 60

Governing a nation is like frying small fish—handle with care.

Approach the world with the Dao,

And evil will find no place to dwell.

It's not that evil spirits don't exist,

But they will cause no harm.

Not only will the spirits cause no harm,

The master will also cause no harm.
When the master and the people do not harm each other,
Virtue can be restored and shared among all.

Chapter 61

Superior nations are positioned downstream,
Where heaven and earth converge,
There the feminine remains.
Femininity often overcomes masculinity with calmness,
Maintaining composure is maintaining a low profile.
Thus, when a great nation humbles itself beneath a smaller nation,
It can surpass the smaller nation.
When a small nation humbles itself beneath a great nation,
It can surpass the greater nation.
Therefore, by staying low, one can conquer,
Or by staying low, one can be conquered.
The greatest mistake for a powerful nation is obsession with
    domination,
The critical mistake for a small nation is obsession with asserting
    dominance.
True greatness is achieved only when both desires are met,
Thus, the superior always stay humble.

Chapter 62

The Dao holds the key to all things,
It is the treasure of goodness,
It is the redeemer of evil.
Eloquent words can influence economies,
Respectable actions can win the hearts of the people.
How can one distance themselves from temptation?
Thus, when a leader is chosen,
And officers are appointed,
Though treasures of honor and chariots of pride may be offered,
Nothing compares to offering a vision rooted in the Dao.

Why is the value of the Dao cherished eternally?
Because it provides without being asked,
And forgives even the gravest sins.
That is why it is cherished by the world.

Chapter 63

Act without acting,
Work without working,
Taste without tasting.
Enlarge the small, increase the diminished,
Reward condemnation with Virtue.
Complexity arises from simplicity,
Greatness is found in the trivial.
Difficult problems must be solved through simplicity,
Great achievements are built on small steps.
Thus, the master remains unconcerned with grand deeds,
And is therefore capable of achieving greatness.
Light promises draw few believers,
The more you simplify, the more complexity arises.
Thus, the master addresses complexity,
And continually avoids complications.

Chapter 64

What is settled is easily maintained,
What is without form is easily planned,
What is fragile is easily broken,
What is small is easily scattered.
Act on it before it materializes,
Manage it before it becomes chaotic.
A towering tree grows from a tiny sprout;
A sky-reaching tower is built from a modest mound,
A long journey begins with a single step.
Those who act upon things will fail,
Those who cling to things will lose.

The master acts not, thus never fails;
Holds onto nothing, thus never loses.
Amateurs often fail at the brink of success.
Stay focused at the end as in the beginning,
And there will be no failure.
Thus, the master desires without attachment,
Values no precious possessions.
Learn to unlearn,
Free the people from their past.
Assist all things in returning to their essence,
And dare not to intervene.

Chapter 65

The timeless masters of the Dao
Do not seek to enlighten the people with it,
But rather to humble them with it.
The people are complex,
Govern them by tempering their intelligence.
To rule a nation with intelligence is to invite betrayal,
To rule without relying on intelligence is to bring blessings to a
    nation.
Understand these two, and set them as guiding principles.
Being wise in setting these standards
Is to possess intricate Virtue.
This intricate Virtue is profound and far-reaching,
Contrary to what it governs, yet leading to peacefulness and
    harmony.

Chapter 66

Lakes and oceans can be the masters of all streams
Because they are good at staying low,
Thus they can be masters of all streams.
So, one who desires to be honored
Must speak humbly of oneself;

One who desires to lead must keep themselves behind.
Thus, the master is above, yet the people do not feel burdened,
Is in front, yet the people do not feel pushed aside.
Therefore, the world gladly pushes the master forward
Without feeling displaced.
Because the master does not contend,
They remain uncontested.
The world says the Dao is great, but it seems useless.
I say that it is great precisely because it seems useless.
If it appeared to be useful,
Its greatness would have diminished over time.

Chapter 67

I have three precious things that I hold dear and cherish.
The first is called mercy,
The second is called prudence,
The third is not daring to be above the world.
With mercy, one can be truly courageous;
With prudence, one can be truly generous;
Not daring to be on top of the world,
One can become a true leader, both influential and respected.
Without mercy, yet seeking courage,
Without prudence, yet seeking generosity,
Without reservation, yet pushing ahead—this is futile!
With mercy, battles are won,
Defense is secured,
The heavens will come to your aid,
And grant protection in its mercy.

Chapter 68

Great gladiators are not violent,
Great warriors are not driven by rage,
Great champions remain uncontested,
Great leaders act with humility.

This is the Virtue of not contesting,
This is the strength of true leadership,
This is the ultimate unity with timelessness.

Chapter 69

There is a saying on the battlefield:
"Dare not be the host, and thus be the guest,
Dare not advance an inch, and thus retreat a foot."
This means to move without moving,
Be armed without weapons,
Cast out without casting,
And be forceful without force.
There is no greater fault than underestimating one's opponent,
To underestimate an opponent is to lose one's caution.
Therefore, when forces clash,
Those who remain reserved are victorious!

Chapter 70

These words are easy to understand and easy to follow,
Yet for worldly people, none can understand, none can follow.
Words create legends,
Deeds create heroes.
Because there is nothing to be known in this, it remains unknown.
Those who know are rare, and those who live by it are worthy of
    respect.
Thus, the master wears humility outwardly and keeps treasures in
    the heart.

Chapter 71

Knowing that you do not know is true wisdom;
Not knowing that you lack this knowledge is a flaw.
Only by recognizing and correcting flaws
Can one be free from defectiveness.
The master is free from defectiveness,

Because they acknowledge and correct their flaws,
Thus, they remain without defectiveness.

Chapter 72

When the people are not threatened by imposing authority,
Authority is imposed without intruding on their lives,
Without belittling their creations.
Because there is no belittling,
There is no resentment.
Thus, the master is introspective and does not proclaim;
Self-loving, but not self-righteous.
Therefore, they are free and at peace.

Chapter 73

Courage in daring brings death,
Courage in not daring brings life.
These two can be favorable or harmful, depending on the
    moment.
What the heavens detest,
Who can truly know?
Thus, the master approaches the complexity with care.
The heavenly Dao:
Contend not and master victory,
Speak not and master oration,
Summon not and things come naturally,
Be honest and master cunning.
The heavenly net is vast and wide,
Its mesh may seem loose, but nothing escapes its reach.

Chapter 74

When people are not afraid of death,
Why threaten them with it?
If someone causes the people to live in constant fear of death,

And bewilders them with confusion, they must be seized and
    executed—
But who would dare?
There are natural executioners who carry out this task,
But those who take the executioner's role upon themselves,
Are like taking the carpenter's job to carve wood.
Those who take the carpenter's job to carve wood,
Seldom avoid cutting their own hands.

Chapter 75

The people's poverty
Is caused by the parasitic exploitation of their superiors,
Thus, there is poverty.
The people's complexity
Is caused by the ambitions of their superiors,
Thus, there is complexity.
The people's willingness to sacrifice
Is due to the weight placed on life,
Thus, there are sacrifices.
Only those who are not ambitious for worldly achievements
Are truly capable of appreciating life.

Chapter 76

People are born gentle and fragile,
They die stiff and tough.
The myriad things, plants and trees, are born tender and fresh,
They die dried and withered.
Thus, those who are stiff and tough are followers of death,
Those who are gentle and fragile are followers of life.
When the armed forces are strong, the nation does not succeed,
When resources are forceful, the arms grow naturally powerful.
True strength comes from staying humble,
Superiority is achieved through gentleness and fragility.

Chapter 77

The heavenly Dao
Is like an arching bow!
What is high is brought low,
What is low is lifted high.
The excessive is diminished,
The lacking is replenished.
The way of the Dao is heavenly,
It supplements the deprived at the expense of the excessive.
The way of the people is different,
They give to the excessive and take from the deprived.
How, then, can there be any excess to offer to the world?
There is none but the Dao.
Thus, the master acts without presumption,
Accomplishes without dwelling on achievements,
And is free from the desire to display their abilities!

Chapter 78

Of all gentleness and submissiveness in the world,
Nothing compares to water.
In tackling stiffness and toughness, nothing is better,
And nothing can easily replace it.
By being submissive, one overcomes dominance,
By being gentle, one overcomes toughness.
Everyone in the world knows this,
Yet few are able to follow it.
Therefore, the master says:
"Accepting the nation's shame is being truly noble;
Accepting the nation's hardships is being truly majestic."
Righteous words often seem contradictory.

Chapter 79

When hateful hostility is resolved,
There will still be lingering resentment.

How can this be cured?
Thus, the master holds onto agreements,
Without blaming anyone.
Those with Virtue focus on working out agreements,
Those without Virtue focus on scrutinizing disagreements.
The Dao is impartial,
It always brings healing to the people.

Chapter 80

A small nation with a small population,
Even without advanced tools or technologies,
The people would rather stay than migrate elsewhere.
Though there are vessels and vehicles for travel,
No one feels the need to use them.
Though there are national guards,
They do not line up for inspection.
People return to simple ways, measuring with straps and knots.
They fulfill their desires and aspirations,
Adorn their clothing,
Secure their homes and quarters,
And find comfort in their beliefs and customs.
Even if the neighboring nation is within sight,
And the sounds of roosters and dogs can be heard,
The people live out their lives without any desire to serve or
    engage with the other nation.

Chapter 81

Truthful words are not always pleasant,
And pleasant words are not always trustworthy.
Those who are good do not argue,
And those who are argumentative are not good.
Those who truly know are not necessarily learned,
And those who are learned may not truly know.
The Sage does not hoard possessions;

The more he does for others, the more he has.
The more he gives, the more he gains.
The Way of Heaven
Is to benefit without causing harm.
The Way of the Sage
Is to act without contention.

Self Reliance

Ralph Waldo Emerson

Self Reliance

"Don't look outside yourself for answers."

"Man is his own guide, and the soul that can live honestly and perfectly commands all light, influence, and fate. Nothing comes too early or too late for him. Our actions are like angels, good or bad, our constant companions.

Throw the child onto the rocks, feed him with the she-wolf's milk; if he grows up with the hawk and the fox, power and speed will be his hands and feet."

~ Ralph Waldo Emmerson

Recently, I read some original poems by a well-known painter. The soul always finds something meaningful in such lines, no matter the topic. The feeling they bring is often more important than any single idea in them. Believing in your own thoughts and trusting that what feels true to you deep down is true for everyone—that is genius. Speak your hidden beliefs, and they can become universal truths; eventually, our deepest thoughts return to us like a final judgment.

The voice of our mind is familiar to each of us. We admire people like Moses, Plato, and Milton because they ignored other people's ideas and books. They didn't repeat what others said; they spoke what they truly thought. We need to learn to recognize the spark of insight that comes from within us, even more than the brilliance of poets and philosophers. But we often push away our thoughts just because they're ours. In every great work, we see our own dismissed ideas coming back to us with a grand, powerful feeling. Great art teaches us to hold onto our first impressions, especially when everyone else disagrees. Otherwise, someday, a stranger will say what we've always felt, and we'll be embarrassed to agree with them.

There comes a time in everyone's life when they see that jealousy is foolish, and copying others is like losing your true self. We have to accept ourselves, with all our strengths and weaknesses, as the share we've been given in life. Although the world is full of good things, nothing worthwhile will come to us unless we work hard on the part we're given to care for. The power inside each of us is unique, and only we know what we can do, but even we don't fully know until we try. Certain faces, people, or events make a deep impression on us, while others do not. This memory isn't random but part of a larger harmony. Our eyes are placed where they are to catch a certain light. We only express part of who we are and feel ashamed of the special idea that each of us represents. If we share our thoughts honestly, we can trust they will lead to good results, but God doesn't show His work through cowards. A person feels truly happy and at peace when they put their heart into their work and do their best; otherwise, they find no rest. Their creativity leaves them, and they find no support or inspiration.

Trust yourself: everyone feels the strength that comes from self-confidence. Accept the place that has been given to you by divine guidance, the society of your time, and the flow of events. Great people have always done this, trusting in the spirit of their time, feeling that the most trustworthy thing is what's in their hearts, guiding their hands and filling their being. We must embrace this same great destiny, not as children or weaklings hiding in a safe corner, nor as cowards running from change, but as guides, helpers, and redeemers, following the will of God and pushing forward against chaos and darkness.

Nature gives us wonderful examples of this truth in the faces and actions of children, infants, and even animals! Their minds aren't divided or uncertain; they don't doubt a feeling just because their calculations disagree with it. Their minds are whole, their eyes bold, and when we look at their faces, we feel disarmed. Infants don't adjust to anyone; all people adjust to them, so often one baby will make four or five adults play and babble. God has given youth, puberty, and adulthood their own charm, making them desirable and kind, and their needs undeniable if they stand on their own. Don't think that a young person has no power because they can't speak to you and me.

Listen! In the next room, their voice is clear and strong. It seems they know how to talk to their peers. Whether shy or bold, they'll know how to make us adults unnecessary.

Boys who are sure of their next meal carry themselves with the free spirit of human nature. A boy in the living room is like an audience in a theater: independent, not responsible, observing people and events as they happen. He judges them fairly and quickly, like boys do, as good, bad, interesting, silly, eloquent, or annoying. He never worries about consequences or personal interests; he gives an honest, independent opinion. You must seek his favor; he doesn't need yours. But adults are like prisoners, trapped by their own awareness. Once they speak or act successfully, they become tied to it, watched by the kindness or anger of many, whose opinions now matter to them. There's no escaping this. Oh, if only they could go back to being neutral! Whoever can stay free from all ties and, after seeing, can see again with the same innocent, unbiased, and fearless spirit, will always be a force. They would speak on all matters passing by, and their words would be seen as essential rather than personal, creating awe among people.

These are the voices we hear when we are alone, but they vanish when we join society. Everywhere, society works against each person's individuality. Society is like a shared company where people agree to give up their freedom and growth in exchange for the comfort of their basic needs. The main virtue it demands is conformity. Society doesn't value reality and creativity but only follows names and customs.

To truly be yourself, you must reject conformity. To reach greatness, don't let so-called "goodness" hold you back; instead, question if it's truly good. The only thing that should be sacred to you is the integrity of your mind. Be true to yourself, and the world will support you. I remember an answer I gave when I was young to a respected advisor who always pressed me with the old doctrines of the church. When I said, "Why should I care about the sacredness of traditions if I live completely from within?" my friend warned, "But these impulses might come from below, not above." I replied, "They don't feel that way to me; but if I'm a child of the Devil, then I'll live from the Devil." No law is sacred to me except the law of my own nature. Good and bad are only labels that can be easily applied to anything; the only right is what agrees with my nature, and the only wrong is what goes against it. A person should carry themselves as though everything else is temporary and fleeting, except for themselves. I am ashamed of how easily we bow to titles and names, to large organizations and outdated systems. Every polite, well-spoken person influences me more than they should. I should stand firm and speak bluntly, expressing the full truth at all times. If spite and pride hide behind kindness, should that go unnoticed? If an angry fanatic claims the noble cause of Abolition and comes to me with his latest news from overseas, why shouldn't I say to him: "Go love your own child; love your neighbor; be kind and modest; show that goodness; and stop hiding your harsh, selfish ambition behind this false concern for people far away. Your distant love is just hidden spite at home." Such a statement might sound rough and unrefined, but truth is more appealing than fake love. Your goodness must have some strength in it, or it is worthless. When love becomes weak and whiny, then hatred must be taught as a balance. I avoid even my father, mother, wife, and brother when my true calling summons me. I would write on my doorpost: Whim. I hope it's more than whim in the end, but we can't spend time explaining. Don't expect me to justify why I choose certain company or avoid others. And don't, as a good man did today, tell me about my duty to place every poor person in a better situation. Are they my poor? I tell you, foolish philanthropist, I begrudge the dollar, the dime, the cent I give to people who aren't connected to me and to whom I am not connected. There is a group of people I'm spiritually linked to; for them, I would go to jail if needed. But as for your random charities, college for the foolish, meeting houses for showy purposes, alms to drunkards, and endless Relief Societies—though I sometimes give the dollar out of shame, it's a wicked dollar that I'll one day have the courage to withhold.

Virtues are seen as exceptions, not the standard. People do what is considered a good action, like a brave deed or act of charity, as if paying a fine for failing to show up regularly for a parade. Their good deeds are done as a way to apologize or make up for living in the world, just as sick and insane people pay high fees. Their virtues are simply penances. I don't want to make up for anything; I just want to live. My life is for itself, not for show. I prefer it to be simple and real, not flashy or unstable. I want it to be steady and pleasant, without needing special handling. I ask for proof that you are genuine, and I reject appeals from someone to their actions. I know, for myself, that it makes no difference whether I perform or avoid actions that others see as excellent. I cannot agree to pay for a right that I naturally possess. Small and limited as my talents may be, I exist and don't need extra evidence for my own assurance or the assurance of others.

What I must do is all that matters to me, not what others think I should do. This rule, as tough in practical life as in intellectual life, might be the sole difference between greatness and smallness. It's harder because you'll always find people who think they know your duty better than you do. It's easy to live by the world's opinion; it's easy, in solitude, to live by our own; but the great person is one who, in the middle of a crowd, keeps the independence of solitude with complete peace.

The problem with following customs that feel lifeless to you is that it drains your energy. It wastes your time and muddles who you really are. If you support a church that's lost its spirit, contribute to an empty Bible society, vote with a big political party either for or against the government, or set your table like a bland host, then under all these acts, I struggle to see the real you. So much energy is pulled away from your true life. But if you do your own work, I will see you. Do your work, and you'll strengthen yourself. A person should realize that conformity is like playing a game of blindman's bluff. If I know your group, I already know your argument. I hear a preacher choose one of his church's institutions as his sermon topic. Don't I know right away that he won't say anything new or genuine? Don't I know that, despite the show of questioning, he won't actually question the institution's foundation? I know he's committed to seeing only one side—the accepted side, not as a true individual, but as a parish minister. He's like a lawyer arguing his client's case, and his show of impartiality is the weakest pretense. Most people have tied blindfolds over their eyes and bound themselves to some shared opinion. This conformity doesn't just make them false in a few points; it makes them false in everything. Every truth they tell is slightly off. Their two is not really two, their four not quite four; so every word they say frustrates us, and we don't even know where to begin to correct them. Meanwhile, nature isn't slow to dress us in the uniform of the group we align with. We end up taking on one style of face and body, slowly forming a subtle, foolish look. There's a particular humiliation that never fails to show itself in history; I mean "the foolish face of praise," the forced smile we put on when we're stuck in conversation that doesn't interest us. Our muscles, moved not by true feeling but by stubborn will, tense up on our faces in an unpleasant way.

For nonconformity, the world punishes you with its disapproval. So, a person must learn how to handle sour looks. Strangers might glare at you in public, or friends might look at you oddly in their living rooms. If their scorn came from genuine conviction like yours, you might go home feeling sad; but the sour looks of the crowd, like their cheerful ones, are usually shallow and change with the wind or the latest news. Even so, the discontent of the crowd can feel more intimidating than the anger of officials or scholars. It's easy for a strong person who understands the world to bear the scorn of the educated classes. Their anger is usually restrained and careful, as they are timid and vulnerable themselves. But when their controlled rage mixes with the anger of the masses, when the ignorant and the poor are stirred up, and when the raw brute force at society's bottom starts to growl and scowl, it takes great courage and deep faith to view it as a small matter.

Another fear that stops us from trusting ourselves is our need for consistency—our respect for our past words or actions, because others have no other way to judge us but by our past, and we hesitate to let them down.

But why constantly look over your shoulder? Why drag around this memory, worried you might contradict something you once said in public? If you do contradict yourself, so what? It seems wise to rely on memory as little as possible, even in acts of memory itself, to bring the past into the present for judgment and live fully in the new day. In your philosophy, you may have denied personality to God, yet if your soul feels drawn to Him, surrender to it with all your heart, even if it means picturing God with form and color. Leave behind your theory, like Joseph left his coat in the hand of the harlot, and flee.

A foolish consistency is the worry of small minds, admired by small-minded politicians, philosophers, and ministers. Consistency means nothing to a great soul. You might as well worry about shadows on the wall. Say what you think now in strong words, and tomorrow, say what you think tomorrow in equally strong words, even if it contradicts everything you said today. "Oh, you'll be misunderstood," some might say. But is it really so bad to be misunderstood? Pythagoras was misunderstood, as were Socrates, Jesus, Luther, Copernicus, Galileo, Newton, and every pure, wise spirit that ever lived. To be great is to be misunderstood.

I believe no one can act against their true nature. All their desires and whims are bound by the law of who they are, just as the peaks and valleys of mountains are minor compared to the curve of the Earth. It doesn't matter how you measure or analyze them. Character is like a pattern; read it forward, backward, or across, and it still reads the same. In this simple, humble life in the woods that God has allowed me, let me record my honest thoughts each day without looking ahead or back. I am sure they will form a harmonious pattern, even if I don't try to make it so or even see it happening. My book should smell of pine trees and echo with the sounds of insects. The swallow outside my window should weave the thread or straw he carries in his beak into my work as well. We are seen for what we are.

Character teaches more than our intentions. People think they show their virtue or vice only through obvious actions, not realizing that virtue or vice radiates from them every moment.

There will be harmony in any variety of actions as long as they are honest and natural at the moment. For a single person, actions will be in harmony, even if they seem different. These differences fade when viewed from a higher perspective. One purpose unites them all. The path of the best ship is a zigzag line of many turns. Seen from afar, the line appears straight along its general direction. Your true actions will explain themselves and your other true actions. Conformity explains nothing. Act as an individual, and your past individual actions will justify you now. Greatness looks to the future. If I am firm enough today to do right and ignore opinions, then I must have done enough right before to defend myself now. No matter what happens, do the right thing now. Always disregard appearances, and you'll always be able to. Character builds up power over time. Every day of past virtue strengthens today. What fills the imagination with the greatness of heroes from the senate and battlefield? The awareness of a series of great days and past victories. These cast a united light on the one acting now. He is accompanied by an invisible host of angels. That's what gives power to Chatham's voice, dignity to Washington's stance, and vision to Adams's gaze. Honor is sacred because it isn't fleeting. It always represents ancient virtue. We admire it today because it isn't just for today. We love and honor it because it isn't meant to trap us for our love and honor, but is self-reliant and self-made, with a pure, noble lineage, even when it appears in a young person.

I hope we have seen the last of conformity and consistency in these times. Let these words be mocked from now on. Instead of a dinner gong, let us hear the call of a Spartan flute. Let's stop bowing and apologizing. A great person is coming to dine at my house. I don't want to please him; I want him to want to please me. I will stand here for humanity, and while I'd make it kind, I would also make it true. Let us stand up to the smooth mediocrity and shallow contentment of our time, and throw in the face of custom, trade, and duty the fact that is the essence of all history: that there is a great responsible Thinker and Actor working wherever a person works; a true person belongs to no time or place but stands at the center of all things. Where he is, there is nature. He measures you, all people, and all events. Most people in society remind us of others or something else. But character, reality, reminds you of nothing else; it is above all of creation. A person should be so substantial that circumstances mean nothing to them. Every true person is a cause, a nation, and an era, needing boundless spaces, people, and time to fully realize their purpose—future generations seem to follow them like a procession of loyal followers. When a Caesar is born, we get a Roman Empire for ages. When Christ is born, millions of minds grow and attach themselves to his genius, confusing him with human virtue and potential. An institution is the shadow of one person, as Monasticism is the shadow of Antony the hermit; the Reformation, of Luther; Quakerism, of Fox; Methodism, of Wesley; Abolition, of Clarkson. Milton called Scipio "the height of Rome," and all of history can be understood as the biography of a few strong and devoted individuals.

Let a person understand their own worth and keep everything else in its rightful place, under their feet. Let them not sneak around or act like a beggar, an outsider, or an unwanted guest in a world made for them. Yet the person on the street, finding nothing in themselves that feels equal to the force that built a towering structure or sculpted a marble statue, feels small when looking at these. A palace, a statue, a rare book—all have a distant, intimidating look, like a fine carriage that seems to ask, "Who are you, Sir?" But these things all belong to him, waiting for his attention, asking his abilities to awaken and take possession. The painting waits for my opinion; it doesn't command me. I am the one who judges its value. The popular story of a drunken man found on the street, taken to a duke's house, cleaned, dressed, laid in the duke's bed, and then treated with full ceremony like the duke, being assured he'd been out of his mind, owes its charm to its symbolism of humanity's condition. We, too, are in the world like this drunk, stumbling, but sometimes we wake up, think clearly, and realize our true nobility.

Our reading is humble and often sycophantic. Our imagination tricks us when we read history. Kingdoms, power, and wealth seem grander than the daily lives of ordinary John and Edward in their small homes, but the essence of life is the same for both; the total sum is the same. Why all this reverence for figures like Alfred, Scanderbeg, and Gustavus? Suppose they were virtuous; did they use up all the virtue there is? Your actions today, as a private individual, carry as much weight as the public, celebrated deeds of kings. When private people act with their own views and vision, the glory will shift from the actions of kings to those of common people.

The world has been taught by its kings, who have captured the imaginations of nations. This grand symbol—the king—taught people to respect each other. The deep loyalty with which people have let the king, the noble, or the wealthy walk among them by law, creating their own scale of value, overturning other scales, paying with honor instead of money, and embodying the law in their person, was a symbol by which they hinted, even if dimly, at their own awareness of personal rights and dignity—the rights of every person.

The attraction that original action holds over us becomes clear when we explore the reason for self-trust. Who is the Trustee? What is this original Self, on which universal reliance can be based? What is the essence of that unmeasurable, science-defying light—without angles, without elements—that shines beauty even into trivial or flawed actions if they carry a trace of independence? This search leads us to the source of it all: the force known as Spontaneity or Instinct, the essence of genius, virtue, and life. This fundamental wisdom is called Intuition, while all other teachings are just instructions. In this deep, final power—beyond which nothing else can be analyzed—all things find their common origin. For that sense of existence, which in calm hours rises mysteriously in the soul, is not separate from things, space, light, time, or humanity, but one with them, evidently arising from the same source as their life and existence. We first share in the life by which all things exist, then see them as forms in nature, forgetting that we share in their cause. Here lies the source of thought and action. Here are the lungs of the inspiration that grants humanity wisdom and cannot be denied without irreverence. We lie in the embrace of a vast intelligence, which makes us receivers of its truth and vessels of its actions. When we recognize justice or truth, we aren't doing anything by our own power but allowing a channel for its light to pass through. If we ask where this comes from, if we seek to analyze the soul that causes it, philosophy fails us. All we can affirm is its presence or absence. Each person distinguishes between their mind's voluntary actions and its involuntary perceptions, knowing that perfect faith belongs to these involuntary perceptions. They may make mistakes in expressing them, but they know these things to be as undeniable as day and night. My purposeful actions and achievements are mere wanderings—yet the smallest native feeling, the slightest natural emotion, demands my respect and attention. Thoughtless people easily dismiss perceptions as if they were opinions or random choices, because they don't understand the difference between perception and idea. They assume that I choose to see this or that. But perception is not a whim; it is bound by fate. If I see a trait, my children will see it after me, and eventually, everyone will, even if no one else has noticed it yet. For my perception of it is as real as the sun.

The soul's relationship to the divine spirit is so pure that it is profane to add anything else to it. When God speaks, it must be that He communicates everything, not just one thing; He fills the world with His voice, radiating light, nature, time, and souls from the center of present thought, renewing and recreating all. Whenever a mind is simple and receives divine wisdom, old things pass away—means, teachers, texts, temples fall; it lives now, absorbing past and future into the present moment. All things are made sacred by their connection to it—one thing as much as another. Everything is reduced to its core by its cause, and in the universal miracle, small, specific miracles vanish. Therefore, if someone claims to understand and speak of God but points you back to the language of an ancient, decaying nation in another world, do not believe them. Is the acorn superior to the oak, its fullness and completion? Is the parent better than the child into whom they have poured their mature being? Why, then, this reverence for the past? The ages conspire against the clarity and authority of the soul. Time and space are merely colors produced by the eye, but the soul is light itself; where it is, it is day; where it was, it is night; and history is nothing but an intrusion and a harm if it serves as anything more than a cheerful story of my own existence and growth.

Humanity is timid and apologetic; no longer bold, we don't dare to say, "I think" or "I am," instead quoting some saint or wise figure. We feel embarrassed before a blade of grass or a blooming rose. The roses outside my window don't refer to roses of the past or better roses somewhere else; they are simply what they are, existing with God in the present. Time means nothing to them. Each rose is perfect in every moment of its life. Before a leaf-bud bursts, its whole life is already active; when fully open, it has nothing more; when only a root without leaves, it has nothing less. Its nature is fulfilled, and it fulfills nature in every stage. But humanity delays, or dwells on memories, unable to live in the present. Instead, we look backward with regret or ignore the riches around us while trying to catch a glimpse of the future. We cannot be happy and strong until we live with nature in the present, above time.

This should be easy to understand. Yet even the strongest minds often won't hear God unless He speaks through the words of David, Jeremiah, or Paul. Someday, we won't value a few texts or certain lives so highly. We are like children repeating by memory the sentences of elders and teachers, and later, of the influential figures we meet— carefully recalling their exact words. But as we grow to see things as those people did, we understand their thoughts and are ready to let the words go. At any time, we can speak equally well when needed. If we live truthfully, we'll see truthfully. It's as easy for a strong person to be strong as it is for a weak person to be weak. When we gain new insights, we will gladly clear away old memories as if they were clutter. When someone lives with God, their voice becomes as gentle as the sound of a stream or the rustling of corn.

And now, the highest truth on this subject remains unspoken; it probably can't be said, as all speech is just a distant echo of intuition. The thought, as best as I can express it now, is this: When goodness is near you and you have life within yourself, it doesn't arrive through any familiar path; you won't trace anyone else's footsteps; you won't see any face or hear any name—the way, the thought, the goodness will be entirely fresh and original. It excludes all examples and past experiences. You move away from humanity, not toward it. All people who have ever lived are its forgotten messengers. Both fear and hope fall beneath it. Even hope feels small in comparison. In moments of vision, there's nothing that can be called gratitude, nor exactly joy. The soul, raised above passion, perceives identity and eternal causation, sees the self-existence of Truth and Right, and settles peacefully in knowing that everything is going well. Vast distances in nature—the Atlantic Ocean, the South Sea—or long stretches of time—years, centuries—become meaningless. What I think and feel is the same force underlying all previous stages of life and experience, just as it underlies what I now call life, and what is called death.

Life itself is valuable, not just having lived. Power fades the moment we rest; it exists in the shift from past to new states, in the leap over boundaries, in aiming toward a goal. This single truth disturbs the world: the soul is always becoming; this process endlessly devalues the past, turns all wealth to poverty, all reputation to insignificance, and equalizes saints and rogues alike, brushing aside both Jesus and Judas. Why then speak of self-reliance? As long as the soul is present, there is power—not a passive confidence, but active force. Talking about "reliance" is just a weak, external way of speaking. It's better to speak of that which relies because it acts and exists. Whoever has more obedience to principle than I do will naturally hold authority over me, even without lifting a finger. I must orbit around them, drawn by the pull of spirits. We think we're just using rhetoric when we speak of high virtue. We don't yet understand that virtue is Height, and that any person or group, open and attuned to principles, will inevitably overpower and surpass all cities, nations, kings, wealthy people, poets, who lack that openness.

This is the ultimate realization we reach on every subject: everything resolves into the ever-blessed One. Self-existence is an attribute of the Supreme Cause, marking the measure of good by its degree of presence in all lesser forms. Everything that is real holds its reality through its virtue. Commerce, farming, hunting, whaling, war, eloquence, personal influence—all these reflect its presence and imperfect action, and so they earn my respect. I see the same law working in nature for preservation and growth. Power is, in nature, the essential measure of right. Nature allows nothing to stay in her realm that cannot support itself. The formation and balance of a planet, the tree bending back from a fierce wind, the life force within every animal and plant—all demonstrate a self-sufficient, and thus self-relying, soul.

So everything converges: let us not wander; let us stay close to the source. Let us stun and awe the crowd of people, books, and institutions that intrude by a simple declaration of divine truth. Tell the intruders to remove their shoes, for God is here within us. Let our simplicity judge them, and our commitment to our own law show the poverty of nature and fortune when compared to our own inner riches.

But we have become a mob. People no longer revere each other, nor are they drawn to stay at home to connect with their internal depths; instead, they go out to beg for a mere cup of water from others. We must go alone. I prefer the quiet church before the service starts to any sermon. How distant, how cool, how pure people seem, each surrounded by a sacred space! So let us always sit. Why should I take on the flaws of my friends, family, or children just because we share a home or blood? All people are my kin, and I am kin to all. But for that, I won't adopt their impatience or foolishness, nor will I feel ashamed for it. However, your solitude must not be mechanical but spiritual; it must be uplifted. Sometimes, the whole world seems to conspire to load you with petty concerns. Friends, clients, children, sickness, fear, need, charity—all knock at once, saying, "Come out to us." But keep your state; don't join their confusion. The power others have to disturb us is one we give them through weak curiosity. No one can come close to me except through my own actions. "What we love, we have, but through desire, we deprive ourselves of love."

If we can't immediately rise to the sanctities of obedience and faith, then let us at least resist temptations; let us declare a state of battle and awaken Thor and Woden—courage and determination—in our Saxon hearts. In our calm times, this is done by speaking the truth. End false hospitality and affection. Stop living to fulfill the expectations of these deceived and deceiving people we associate with. Say to them, "O father, O mother, O wife, O brother, O friend, I have lived with you by appearances until now. From now on, I belong to truth." Let it be known that henceforth, I obey no law lesser than the eternal law. I will not make promises, only stand nearby. I will aim to support my parents, provide for my family, and be the faithful husband of one wife, but I must fulfill these relationships in a fresh, unprecedented way. I defy your customs. I must be myself. I can no longer break myself for anyone. If you can love me for who I am, we will be happier. If not, I will still work to deserve your respect. I won't hide my preferences or dislikes. I will trust that what is deep is sacred, doing openly under the sun and moon what satisfies my heart and inner calling. If you are noble, I will love you; if not, I will neither harm you nor deceive myself with false attention. If you are true but not in the same truth as I, stay with your companions; I will seek mine. I do this not selfishly, but sincerely and truthfully. It is in the interest of you, me, and everyone, after living in untruths for so long, to live in truth. Does this sound harsh today? Soon you will love what your nature and mine require, and if we follow truth, it will lead us safely in the end.

But in doing this, you may cause your friends pain. Yes, but I cannot sell my freedom and strength just to protect their feelings. Besides, everyone has moments of reason when they look into the realm of absolute truth; then they will justify my actions and may even do the same themselves.

The masses believe that rejecting popular standards means rejecting all standards, mere lawlessness, and that a bold sensualist uses philosophy's name to excuse his wrongs. But the law of conscience remains. There are two places where we must account for ourselves, and we will confess in one or the other. You may fulfill your obligations by clearing yourself according to the direct or indirect way. Consider whether you have met your duties to your father, mother, cousin, neighbor, town, cat, and dog; whether any of these can find fault with you. But I may also ignore this indirect standard and absolve myself. I have my own stern obligations, my own complete inner circle. It denies the name of duty to many tasks that are usually thought of as duties. But if I can meet its demands, it lets me disregard the common code. If anyone thinks this inner law is easy, let them try obeying it for a single day.

Indeed, it requires something godlike in a person to throw off society's ordinary motives and dare to trust themselves as their own guide. Let their heart be high, their will firm, their vision clear, so that they can sincerely be their own doctrine, their own society, and their own law, where a simple purpose feels as binding as iron to others.

Anyone looking at the current state of what we call society can see the need for these ethics. Humanity's strength and spirit seem to be drained out, leaving us fearful, complaining, and timid. We're afraid of truth, fate, death, and each other. Our age doesn't produce great, complete individuals. We need people who can renew life and society, yet most are unable to meet even their own needs, harboring ambition far beyond their abilities, while constantly asking for support. Our way of life is poor, our arts, trades, marriages, and religion are chosen not by us, but by society. We are mere parlor soldiers. We avoid the tough battles of life, where true strength is born.

If young people fail in their first attempts, they lose hope. If a young merchant fails, they say he's ruined. If the brightest mind graduates from one of our colleges but doesn't secure a position in a city within a year, friends and even they themselves feel justified in feeling defeated and resigned. But a sturdy young man from New Hampshire or Vermont, who tries every profession in turn—driving a team, farming, selling goods, teaching, preaching, editing a paper, entering Congress, buying land, and so on, year after year, always landing on his feet like a cat—is worth a hundred of these city-bred ornaments. He moves through his days with pride, not embarrassed that he hasn't "studied a profession," because he isn't postponing his life; he's already living it. He has not one chance, but a hundred. Let a Stoic come forward to reveal humanity's potential and tell people that they are not weak, clinging vines, but can and must stand on their own; that with self-trust, new abilities will emerge; that each person is a living word, meant to uplift nations, that they should be ashamed of our pity, and that once they act from within, throwing away rules, books, idols, and traditions, we pity them no longer, but admire and respect them. Such a teacher would restore life's splendor to humanity and make their name beloved in history.

It's clear that greater self-reliance would bring about a revolution in all of life's roles and relationships—in people's religion, education, work, ways of living, associations, property, and even their philosophies.

What prayers people indulge in! What they call a holy act is neither brave nor strong. Prayer turns outward, asking for some external addition or foreign virtue, losing itself in endless complexities of the natural and supernatural, mediatorial, and miraculous. Prayer that begs for a specific benefit—anything less than all goodness—is flawed. True prayer is contemplating life's facts from the highest viewpoint. It is the monologue of a watching, rejoicing soul. It is the spirit of God announcing His works as good. But using prayer as a way to get a private benefit is mean and dishonest. It assumes dualism, not the unity of nature and consciousness. When a person is truly one with God, they will no longer beg. They will then see prayer in every action. The farmer's prayer is in kneeling to weed his field; the rower's prayer is in each pull of the oar. These are true prayers heard by nature, even if they are for simple purposes. In Fletcher's *Bonduca*, Caratach, when advised to seek guidance from the god Audate, replies,—

"His hidden meaning lies in our efforts; our courage is our best god."

Another type of false prayer is regret. Discontent reflects a lack of self-reliance; it is a weakness of will. Regret calamities if you can help those who suffer; if not, focus on your work, and already the harm begins to mend. Our sympathy is just as flawed. We approach those who mourn senselessly and sit down to cry with them, instead of offering truth and health like a shock of energy that would reconnect them to reason. The secret of good fortune is joy in our own hands. The self-reliant person is always welcome among both gods and people. For him, every door opens: all tongues greet him, all honors are given, and all eyes follow him with admiration. We love him because he does not need our love. We carefully and humbly celebrate him because he stayed true to himself and disregarded our disapproval. The gods love him because people resented him. "To the persevering mortal," said Zoroaster, "the blessed Immortals are swift."

Just as people's prayers show weakness of will, so do their beliefs show weakness of mind. They echo the foolish words of the Israelites, "Let not God speak to us, lest we die. Speak thou, any man, and we will obey." Everywhere I am prevented from meeting God in my brother because he has closed his own temple doors, repeating only what he learned from his brother's or his ancestors' God. Every original mind brings a new perspective. If it proves a mind of rare energy and depth—a Locke, a Lavoisier, a Hutton, a Bentham, a

Fourier—it imposes its classification on others, creating a new system. The greater the depth of thought and the number of insights it reaches, the more satisfaction it brings to those who learn from it. This satisfaction is most evident in religious creeds and doctrines, classifications created by some powerful mind interpreting basic truths about duty and humanity's relationship to the Highest. Such are Calvinism, Quakerism, and Swedenborgianism. The learner finds joy in fitting everything into the new language, like a girl who has just learned botany, discovering a new world of plants and seasons. For a time, the learner feels empowered by studying the mind of their master. But in all unbalanced minds, the classification becomes an idol, seen as the goal rather than a limited tool, so that the system's walls appear to merge with the universe itself; the stars seem hung on the arch their teacher built. They cannot imagine how outsiders could see anything else—"You must have somehow stolen this light from us." They do not yet realize that untamed, uncontainable light will enter any home, even their own. Let them chirp for a while and call the light their own. If they are honest and work well, their tidy enclosure will soon prove too narrow and low; it will crack, lean, rot, and fade, while the immortal light, forever young and joyful, will shine with endless colors across the universe, as it did on the first morning.

The obsession with travel, with places like Italy, England, and Egypt as its idols, still captivates educated Americans, likely because they lack a true sense of self. The people who made England, Italy, or Greece legendary in our minds did so by staying rooted in one place, like an anchor of the earth. In moments of strength, we understand that duty is where we belong. The soul is not meant to wander; the wise person stays home, and even when duty or necessity calls them to other lands, they still carry home within them. They show, by their demeanor, that they travel as someone in control, not as a mere visitor or servant.

I have no problem with going around the world for art, study, or kindness, as long as the person remains grounded and isn't looking for something beyond what they already know. Someone who travels for fun or to find something they're missing only moves further away from themselves, growing old even in youth among things that are already old. In Thebes, in Palmyra, their will and mind become as ancient and worn-out as the ruins they see. They bring ruins to ruins.

Traveling is an illusion. Our first trips show us how indifferent places are to us. At home, I imagine being overwhelmed by beauty in Naples, in Rome, leaving behind my sadness. I pack my things, say goodbye to my friends, set out, and finally arrive in Naples, only to face the same unchanging truth: the same self, still the same, the one I tried to escape. I visit the Vatican and the grand palaces. I pretend to be thrilled by the sights and the ideas they inspire, but deep down, I am not. My burden, my giant, follows me wherever I go.

The urge to travel points to a deeper restlessness of the mind. Our intellect tends to wander, and our education encourages this restlessness. Our minds roam even when our bodies stay at home. We imitate, and isn't imitation just mental travel? Our homes show foreign influences; our shelves hold decorations from distant lands; our views, tastes, and skills lean toward what's far away and long ago. The soul inspired art wherever it blossomed. Artists found their models in their own minds, applying their thoughts to the task at hand. Why must we copy the Doric or Gothic style? Beauty, practicality, depth of thought, and expression are just as available to us as to anyone else, and if the American artist works with hope and dedication, taking into account the climate, the land, the hours of sunlight, the needs of the people, and the form of government, they will create a building that fits all of these, satisfying both taste and feeling.

Rely on yourself; never imitate. Your unique talent comes with the power of a lifetime's growth, but when you adopt someone else's skills, you only gain a temporary, limited ability. What each of us does best, only our Creator can teach us. No one knows what that is, nor can know, until it's shown. Who could have taught Shakespeare? Who could have guided Franklin, or Washington, or Bacon, or Newton?

Every great person is unique. What made Scipio special was exactly what he couldn't borrow. Shakespeare won't be created by studying Shakespeare. Do the work assigned to you, and you can dream and strive as much as you wish. There is a bold and noble expression meant for you, different from the mighty chisel of Phidias, the bricks of the Egyptians, the pen of Moses, or Dante, yet distinct from all of these. The soul, rich and expressive with its many voices, won't repeat itself; but if you listen to what these ancient voices say, you can respond in that same spirit, for listening and speaking are two sides of the same nature. Stay true to your simple, honorable place, follow your heart, and you will create a new world.

Just as our religion, education, and art look outward, so does our social nature. Everyone takes pride in society's progress, yet no one personally improves.

Society never truly moves forward. It loses on one side as quickly as it gains on the other. It constantly changes; it can be barbaric, civilized, Christian, wealthy, scientific—but change is not the same as improvement. With every gain, something is lost. Society acquires new skills but loses old instincts. Compare the well-dressed, literate, thoughtful American with a watch, pencil, and bank notes in his pocket to the naked New Zealander, whose possessions are a club, a spear, a mat, and a shared piece of a shelter. But if you compare their health, you'll see that the modern man has lost his original strength. An honest traveler would notice that a deep wound on the native would heal in days, like soft pitch, while the same injury would kill the modern man.

The modern person has made a coach but lost the use of his feet. He relies on crutches but lacks the support of his own muscles. He has an expensive Geneva watch but can't tell time by the sun. He trusts a nautical almanac from Greenwich to give him information, yet he doesn't recognize a single star in the sky. He knows nothing of the solstice or the equinox, and the entire brilliant calendar of the year is empty in his mind. His notebooks weaken his memory; his libraries overwhelm his wisdom; the insurance office actually leads to more accidents. We might even wonder if machinery doesn't hold us back, if we've lost strength through comfort, the energy of untamed virtue through organized Christianity. For in ancient times, every Stoic truly lived as a Stoic; but in Christian society, where is the Christian?

There is no more variation in moral character than in height or size. No greater people exist today than in the past. There is a certain equality between the great individuals of early times and those of today; not even all the science, art, religion, and philosophy of the nineteenth century can create greater people than the heroes of Plutarch, who lived twenty-four centuries ago. Human progress is not bound to time. Phocion, Socrates, Anaxagoras, and Diogenes were remarkable individuals, but they left no group in their likeness. A person who belongs in their class would not be called by their name but would be entirely their own, becoming a founder of their own group in time. The arts and inventions of each age are like costumes; they don't make people stronger. The harm of advanced machinery may even outweigh its benefits. Hudson and Bering performed remarkable feats in simple fishing boats, surprising Parry and Franklin, whose equipment used the full resources of science and art. With just a simple opera glass, Galileo discovered more wonders in the sky than anyone else. Columbus found the New World in a small, open boat. It's strange to see how tools and machines that were once celebrated gradually fall out of use and decay. The true genius returns to the basics of humanity. We once thought improvements in warfare were among the triumphs of science, yet Napoleon conquered Europe with little more than camps and sheer courage, shedding unnecessary aids. The Emperor believed, as Las Casas reports, that a perfect army would be impossible "without getting rid of weapons, supply depots, and transport, until soldiers, like the Romans, received grain, ground it by hand, and baked bread themselves."

Society is like a wave. The wave moves forward, but the water making it up does not. The same particle doesn't rise from the valley to the crest. Its unity is just an illusion. Today's people of a nation will die within a year, and their experiences vanish with them.

In this way, reliance on property—including governments that protect it—comes from a lack of self-reliance. People have focused on possessions for so long that they have come to view religious, educational, and civil institutions as guardians of property, fearing attacks on them as attacks on property itself. They measure worth by what they have, not by what they are. But a person who cultivates themselves grows ashamed of mere property, finding worth in their own nature. They especially dislike what is accidental—inherited, given as a gift, or even wrongly gained; then they feel it's not truly theirs, just something lying there because no revolution or thief has taken it yet. What a person really is always draws what they need, a living possession beyond the reach of governments, mobs, revolutions, fires, storms, or bankruptcies, constantly renewing wherever they are. "Your share in life," said Caliph Ali, "will come to you, so stop seeking it." Our dependence on foreign goods leads to a blind respect for numbers. Political parties gather in conventions; the larger the crowd, and with each new announcement, "The delegation from Essex! The Democrats from New Hampshire! The Whigs of Maine!" the young patriot feels encouraged by the support of a thousand eyes and hands. Likewise, reformers gather conventions, taking votes and making decisions as a crowd. But that is not the way, friends! The divine presence will enter and reside within you only by the opposite approach. Only as a person lets go of outside support and stands alone do I see them grow strong and successful. Each new follower weakens them. Isn't one person worth more than a town? Expect nothing from others, and while everything around you changes, you, the one firm pillar, will support all that surrounds you. One who knows their inner strength, who weakens from searching for good outside themselves, who throws themselves without hesitation onto their own thoughts, immediately finds balance, stands tall, controls their actions, and works wonders; just as a person standing on their own two feet is stronger than one trying to balance on their head.

Therefore, make use of all that's called Fortune. Most people take chances with her, gaining and losing as her wheel spins. But consider those gains as undeserved, and instead rely on Cause and Effect, the laws of God. Work and achieve in line with your Will, and you chain the wheel of Chance, freeing yourself from its spins. A political victory, a raise in rent, someone recovering from illness, the return of a friend, or any other fortunate event lifts your spirits, and you think good times are on the way. Don't believe it. Nothing can bring you peace but yourself. Nothing can bring you peace but the victory of your own principles.

As A Man Thinketh

James Allen

Introduction

"Mind is the Master power that moulds and makes,
And Man is Mind, and evermore he takes
The tool of Thought, and, shaping what he wills,
Brings forth a thousand joys, a thousand ills:—
He thinks in secret, and it comes to pass:
Environment is but his looking-glass."

~ James Allen

This little book, which is the result of meditation and experience, is not meant to be a complete work on the often-discussed topic of the power of thought. Instead, it aims to inspire rather than explain, with the goal of encouraging men and women to discover and understand the truth that—

"They themselves are makers of themselves."

This is because of the thoughts they choose and nurture. The mind is the master-weaver, shaping both the inner garment of character and the outer garment of circumstance. Although people may have woven their lives in ignorance and pain before, they can now weave in enlightenment and happiness.

James Allen
Broad Park Avenue,
Ilfracombe,

Chapter 1

Thought and Character

The saying "As a man thinks in his heart, so is he" describes not only a person's entire being but also covers every aspect of their life. A person is truly what they think, as their character is the sum total of all their thoughts.

Just as a plant grows from a seed and cannot exist without it, every action of a person comes from hidden seeds of thought and could not happen without them. This applies to actions that seem "spontaneous" and "unpremeditated" as much as it does to those that are planned.

Action is the blossom of thought, and joy and suffering are its fruits. Thus, a person harvests the sweet and bitter outcomes of their own cultivation.

"Thought in the mind has made us what we are. By thought was wrought and built. If a man's mind has evil thoughts, pain comes to him just as the wheel follows the ox. If one endures in purity of thought, joy follows him like his own shadow—sure."

A person grows by law, not by artificial means, and cause and effect are as absolute and unchanging in the hidden realm of thought as they are in the world of visible and material things. A noble and godlike character is not a gift or a result of chance but is the natural result of consistent right thinking and the effect of dwelling on godlike thoughts for a long time. In the same way, an ignoble and beastly character results from continually harboring lowly thoughts.

A person is made or unmade by themselves. In the workshop of thought, they create the weapons that can destroy themselves or the tools with which they build heavenly mansions of joy, strength, and peace. By choosing the right thoughts and applying them correctly, a person rises to divine perfection; by misusing and wrongly applying thoughts, they fall below the level of a beast. Between these two extremes are all the levels of character, and a person is their creator and master.

Of all the beautiful truths about the soul that have been discovered and brought to light in this age, none is more uplifting or full of divine promise and confidence than this: that a person is the master of their thoughts, the shaper of their character, and the creator of their conditions, environment, and destiny.

As a being of power, intelligence, and love, and the ruler of their own thoughts, a person holds the key to every situation and possesses within themselves the transformative and regenerative ability to become what they desire.

A person is always the master, even in their weakest and most abandoned state. However, in their weakness and degradation, they are a foolish master who mismanages their "household." When they begin to reflect on their condition and diligently search for the Law upon which their being is founded, they become the wise master, directing their energies with intelligence and shaping their thoughts to achieve positive outcomes. This is the conscious master, and a person can only become this by discovering within themselves the laws of thought. This discovery is entirely a matter of application, self-analysis, and experience.

Gold and diamonds are obtained only through much searching and mining, and a person can find every truth related to their being if they dig deep into the mine of their soul. They can prove that they are the maker of their character, the shaper of their life, and the builder of their destiny if they watch, control, and change their thoughts, observing their effects on themselves, on others, and on their life and circumstances. By linking cause and effect through patient practice and investigation, and using every experience, even the most trivial, everyday occurrences, as a means of gaining self-knowledge, they gain understanding, wisdom, and power. In this pursuit, like no other, the law is absolute that "He that seeks, finds; and to him that knocks, it shall be opened;" for only through patience, practice, and constant persistence can a person enter the Door of the Temple of Knowledge.

Chapter 2

Effect of Thought on Circumstances

A man's mind can be compared to a garden, which can be carefully tended or allowed to grow wild. But whether you take care of it or not, it will produce something. If you don't plant good seeds, weeds will grow in abundance.

Just as a gardener takes care of his garden, keeping it free from weeds and growing the flowers and fruits he wants, a person can tend the garden of their mind by removing wrong, useless, and impure thoughts and nurturing right, useful, and pure ones. By doing this, a person eventually realizes that they are the master gardener of their soul and the director of their life. They also discover the laws of thought within themselves and understand more clearly how thoughts shape their character, circumstances, and destiny.

Thought and character are connected, and since character shows itself through environment and circumstances, a person's outer conditions will always be related to their inner state. This doesn't mean that a person's circumstances at any moment fully reveal their entire character, but that these circumstances are deeply linked to some essential thought within them and are necessary for their growth at that time.

Every person is where they are because of the law of their being. The thoughts they have built into their character have brought them there, and nothing in their life happens by chance. Everything is the result of a law that cannot make mistakes. This is true for both those who feel out of harmony with their surroundings and those who are content.

As a growing and evolving being, a person is where they are to learn and grow. As they learn the spiritual lesson in any circumstance, it passes away and makes room for new ones.

People are affected by circumstances as long as they believe they are controlled by outside conditions. But when they realize they are a creative force and can control the inner seeds and soil from which circumstances grow, they become the true master of themselves.

Anyone who has practiced self-control and self-purification knows that circumstances arise from thought. They notice that changes in their circumstances occur in exact proportion to their mental changes. When someone sincerely works to fix their character's flaws and makes quick and noticeable progress, they often go through a series of changes.

The soul attracts what it secretly harbors, loves, and fears. It reaches the heights of its aspirations and falls to the level of its unrefined desires, and circumstances are how the soul receives its due.

Every thought planted in the mind takes root, grows into action, and bears fruit in the form of opportunity and circumstance. Good thoughts bring good fruit; bad thoughts bring bad fruit.

The external world shapes itself to the internal world of thought. Both pleasant and unpleasant conditions ultimately benefit the individual. As a harvester of his own crop, a person learns through both suffering and joy.

By following the desires, aspirations, and thoughts that dominate him—whether pursuing fleeting fantasies or steadfastly following the path of high endeavor—a person ultimately reaches their fulfillment in the outer conditions of their life. Everywhere, the laws of growth and adjustment apply.

A person does not end up in poverty or jail because of fate or circumstance but by following lowly thoughts and desires. Similarly, a pure-minded person does not suddenly commit a crime due to external forces; the criminal thought was nurtured in their heart long before, and opportunity revealed its power. Circumstance does not make the man; it reveals him to himself. One cannot fall into vice without vicious inclinations or rise into virtue without nurturing virtuous aspirations. As the lord of thought, a person makes himself, shaping his environment and destiny. Even at birth, the soul attracts the conditions that reflect its purity and impurity, strength and weakness.

People do not attract what they want but what they are. Their whims and ambitions are thwarted, but their innermost thoughts and desires are fulfilled, whether good or bad. The "divinity that shapes our ends" is within us; it is our very self. Only a person can chain themselves. Thought and action are the jailers of fate, imprisoning us when base and liberating us when noble. A person does not receive what they wish and pray for, but what they earn. Their wishes and prayers are fulfilled only when they align with their thoughts and actions.

In light of this truth, what does it mean to "fight against circumstances"? It means continually opposing an external effect while nurturing and maintaining its cause in one's heart. This cause may be a conscious vice or an unconscious weakness, but it hinders progress and calls for remedy.

People want to improve their circumstances but are unwilling to improve themselves, so they remain stuck. A person who does not shy away from self-sacrifice will always achieve their goals. This applies to both earthly and heavenly pursuits. Even someone who wants to become wealthy must be willing to make personal sacrifices to succeed. How much more must one do to achieve a balanced and strong life?

Consider a man who is desperately poor. He wants to improve his surroundings and comfort but shirks his work and thinks he is justified in deceiving his employer due to low wages. Such a man does not understand the basic principles of prosperity and is not only unable to rise out of poverty but attracts deeper misery by indulging in lazy and deceptive thoughts.

Or consider a wealthy man who suffers from a persistent disease caused by gluttony. He is willing to spend large sums to cure it but won't give up his excessive desires. He wants to enjoy rich food and good health, but he is unfit for health because he hasn't learned the basics of a healthy life.

Then there is the employer who cuts wages to increase profits, not realizing he is setting himself up for failure. When he faces bankruptcy in both reputation and wealth, he blames circumstances, not knowing he is the sole author of his condition.

These examples illustrate that a person often unconsciously creates their circumstances. While aiming for a good outcome, they undermine their success by nurturing thoughts and desires that don't align with their goals. Readers can trace the action of thought in their minds and lives and see how external circumstances cannot serve as the sole basis for reasoning.

Circumstances are complex, thought is deeply rooted, and the conditions of happiness vary greatly among individuals. A man's entire soul condition, though it may be known to himself, cannot be judged by another based solely on his external life. A man may be honest in some areas yet suffer privations; a man may be dishonest in some areas yet acquire wealth. The conclusion that one fails due to honesty and the other succeeds due to dishonesty results from superficial judgment, assuming the dishonest man is entirely corrupt and the honest man is entirely virtuous. Deeper knowledge and experience show such judgments to be false. The dishonest man may have virtues the other lacks, and the honest man may have vices the other is free from. The honest man reaps the rewards of his good thoughts and actions and suffers from his vices. The dishonest man similarly experiences his own suffering and happiness.

It's comforting to human vanity to believe one suffers due to virtue, but until a man removes every bitter and impure thought from his mind and cleanses his soul of sin, he cannot declare that his suffering is due to his good qualities. Before reaching supreme perfection, he will find the Great Law of Justice operating in his mind and life, which does not give good for evil or evil for good. With this knowledge, he will look back on his past ignorance and blindness and know that his life is and always has been justly ordered and that all his past experiences, good and bad, were the fair outcomes of his evolving self.

Good thoughts and actions never produce bad results, and bad thoughts and actions never produce good results. Just as corn cannot produce anything but corn and nettles nothing but nettles, this law is understood in the natural world. Still, few understand it in the mental and moral world, though it operates just as consistently there.

Suffering always results from wrong thoughts. It indicates that an individual is out of harmony with themselves and the law of their being. The sole purpose of suffering is to purify and remove all that is useless and impure. Suffering ceases for the pure. There is no reason to burn gold once the impurities have been removed, and a perfectly pure and enlightened being cannot suffer.

The circumstances a man encounters with suffering result from his own mental disharmony. The circumstances a man encounters with blessedness result from his own mental harmony. Blessedness, not material possessions, measures right thought; wretchedness, not a lack of material possessions, measures wrong thought. A man may be cursed and rich, or blessed and poor. Blessedness and riches only come together when riches are rightly and wisely used. A poor man only falls into wretchedness when he sees his situation as an unjust burden.

Poverty and indulgence are the two extremes of wretchedness, both equally unnatural and the result of mental disorder. A man is only rightly conditioned when he is happy, healthy, and prosperous, and happiness, health, and prosperity result from harmoniously aligning his inner self with his surroundings.

A person begins to truly live when they stop complaining and blaming others and start searching for the hidden justice that governs their life. As they align their mind with this justice, they stop blaming others for their condition and build themselves up with strong and noble thoughts. They stop fighting against circumstances and begin to use them to progress faster and discover their inner powers and possibilities.

Law, not chaos, is the dominant principle in the universe; justice, not injustice, is the soul of life; and righteousness, not corruption, is the force behind the spiritual governance of the world. This means that by aligning himself with righteousness, a man will find that the universe aligns with him. As he changes his thoughts towards things and people, things and people will change towards him.

The truth of this is in every person, allowing for easy investigation through introspection and self-analysis. Let a person radically change their thoughts, and they will be amazed at the rapid transformation it brings to their material conditions. People think thoughts can be kept secret, but they can't; thoughts quickly crystallize into habits, which solidify into circumstances. Bestial thoughts lead to habits of drunkenness and sensuality, which result in poverty and disease. Impure thoughts lead to habits of confusion and distraction, resulting in adverse circumstances. Fearful, doubtful, and indecisive thoughts lead to weak habits, resulting in failure and dependence. Lazy thoughts lead to habits of uncleanliness and dishonesty, resulting in poverty. Hateful and critical thoughts lead to habits of accusation and violence, resulting in injury and persecution. Selfish thoughts lead to self-seeking habits, resulting in distressing circumstances. Conversely, beautiful thoughts lead to habits of grace and kindness, resulting in pleasant circumstances. Pure thoughts lead to habits of self-control, resulting in peace. Courageous and self-reliant thoughts lead to successful and free circumstances. Energetic thoughts lead to habits of cleanliness and industry, resulting in pleasant circumstances. Gentle and forgiving thoughts lead to protective circumstances. Loving and selfless thoughts lead to self-forgetfulness habits, resulting in prosperity and true riches.

A particular train of thought, whether good or bad, will inevitably produce results on character and circumstances. While a person cannot directly choose their circumstances, they can choose their thoughts and, by doing so, indirectly shape their circumstances.

Nature helps everyone fulfill the thoughts they most encourage, and opportunities arise that will quickly bring good and evil thoughts to the surface.

Let a person abandon sinful thoughts, and the world will soften towards them and be ready to help. Let them discard weak thoughts, and opportunities will arise to aid their strong resolves. Let them nurture good thoughts, and no hard fate will bind them to wretchedness and shame. The world is your kaleidoscope, and its ever-changing patterns are the carefully adjusted pictures of your thoughts.

"So You will be what you will to be;
Let failure find its false content
In that poor word, 'environment,'
But spirit scorns it, and is free.
"It masters time, it conquers space;
It cowes that boastful trickster, Chance,
And bids the tyrant Circumstance
Uncrown, and fill a servant's place.
"The human Will, that force unseen,
The offspring of a deathless Soul,
Can hew a way to any goal,
Though walls of granite intervene.
"Be not impatient in delays
But wait as one who understands;
When spirit rises and commands
The gods are ready to obey."

Chapter 3

Effect of Thought on Health and the Body

The body serves the mind. It follows what the mind thinks, whether those thoughts are intentionally chosen or come automatically. When the mind is filled with negative or unlawful thoughts, the body quickly falls into sickness and decay. On the other hand, when the mind is full of happy and beautiful thoughts, the body becomes youthful and healthy.

Just like circumstances, disease and health are rooted in thought. Sickly thoughts show up in a sickly body. Fearful thoughts can kill a person as quickly as a bullet, and they are constantly affecting thousands of people, even if not as suddenly. Those who fear disease are the ones who often get it. Anxiety weakens the entire body and makes it susceptible to disease, while impure thoughts, even if not acted upon physically, will eventually harm the nervous system.

Strong, pure, and happy thoughts build up the body with strength and grace. The body is sensitive and responds to the thoughts it receives, and habitual thoughts will have their effects, whether good or bad.

People will continue to have impure and unhealthy bodies as long as they have unclean thoughts. A clean heart leads to a clean life and a healthy body. A polluted mind leads to a corrupt life and an unhealthy body. Thought is the source of action, life, and expression; make the source pure, and everything will be pure.

Changing one's diet won't help if a person doesn't change their thoughts. When a person purifies their thoughts, they no longer desire unhealthy food.

Pure thoughts lead to clean habits. A so-called saint who does not wash is not a saint. A person who strengthens and purifies their thoughts does not need to worry about harmful germs.

To protect your body, guard your mind. To renew your body, beautify your mind. Thoughts of malice, envy, disappointment, and despair rob the body of its health and beauty. A sour face is not an accident; it is created by sour thoughts. Wrinkles are caused by foolishness, passion, and pride.

I know a woman who is ninety-six with the bright, innocent face of a young girl. I know a man who is much younger, yet his face is distorted by passion and discontent. The difference is that the woman has a sweet and sunny disposition, while the man has been consumed by negative emotions.

Just as you cannot have a sweet and healthy home without letting in air and sunshine, you cannot have a strong body and a bright, happy face without letting thoughts of joy, goodwill, and calmness into your mind.

On the faces of the elderly, some wrinkles are made by sympathy, others by pure thought, and others by passion. Who cannot tell the difference? For those who have lived righteously, old age is calm, peaceful, and gently mellowed, like a setting sun. I recently saw a philosopher on his deathbed. He was not old, except in years. He died as sweetly and peacefully as he lived.

Cheerful thoughts are the best medicine for curing the body's ills, and goodwill is the best comfort for dispelling grief and sorrow. Living with thoughts of ill will, cynicism, suspicion, and envy is like being in a prison you've built yourself. But thinking well of others, being cheerful, and finding the good in everyone—such unselfish thoughts are like the gates to heaven. Living each day with thoughts of peace toward all creatures will bring peace to the person who has them.

Chapter 4
Thought and Purpose

Until thought is linked with purpose, there can be no intelligent accomplishment. Most people let their thoughts drift aimlessly through life. Aimlessness is a vice, and anyone who wants to avoid catastrophe and destruction must not let it continue.

Those who lack a central purpose in their lives are easily overwhelmed by worries, fears, troubles, and self-pity, all of which are signs of weakness. These lead to failure, unhappiness, and loss just as surely as deliberately planned sins, though by a different path, because weakness cannot survive in a universe where power is constantly growing.

A person should form a clear purpose in their heart and work towards achieving it. This purpose should become the center of their thoughts. It could be a spiritual ideal or a worldly goal, depending on their nature at the time, but whatever it is, they should consistently focus their mental energy on the goal they have set. This purpose should be their highest priority, and they should dedicate themselves to reaching it, not letting their thoughts wander off into temporary fancies, desires, and imaginings. This is the key to self-control and true concentration of thought. Even if they fail repeatedly to achieve their purpose (as they inevitably will until they overcome their weaknesses), the strength of character they gain will be a true measure of their success. This will become a new starting point for future power and triumph.

Those who are not ready to grasp a great purpose should focus their thoughts on performing their duties flawlessly, no matter how unimportant their tasks may seem. Only in this way can they gather and focus their thoughts, develop resolution and energy, and once this is achieved, there is nothing that cannot be accomplished.

Even the weakest soul, knowing its own weaknesses and believing the truth that strength can only be developed through effort and practice, will begin to exert itself. By adding effort to effort, patience to patience, and strength to strength, it will never stop growing and will eventually become divinely strong.

Just as a physically weak person can become strong through careful and patient training, so can a person with weak thoughts make them strong by practicing right thinking.

To get rid of aimlessness and weakness and to start thinking with purpose is to join the ranks of those strong individuals who only see failure as one of the paths to achievement, who make every condition serve them, and who think strongly, attempt fearlessly, and accomplish masterfully.

Once a person has conceived a purpose, they should mentally map out a direct path to its achievement, without looking to the right or the left. Doubts and fears should be strictly avoided; they are disruptive elements that break up the straight line of effort, making it crooked, ineffective, and useless. Thoughts of doubt and fear have never accomplished anything and never will. They always lead to failure. Purpose, energy, and the power to act disappear when doubt and fear creep in.

The will to act comes from knowing that we can act. Doubt and fear are the greatest enemies of knowledge, and anyone who encourages them or fails to eliminate them hinders themselves at every step.

A person who has conquered doubt and fear has conquered failure. Every thought they have is connected to power, and they face all difficulties bravely and overcome them wisely. Their purposes are planted at the right time, and they bloom and produce fruit, which does not fall prematurely to the ground.

Thought that is fearlessly linked to purpose becomes a creative force: anyone who knows this is ready to become something higher and stronger than a mere bundle of wavering thoughts and fluctuating sensations; anyone who does this has become the conscious and intelligent wielder of their mental powers.

Chapter 5

The Thought-Factor in Achievement

Everything a person achieves or fails to achieve is the direct result of their own thoughts. In a universe that is justly ordered, where any loss of balance would mean total destruction, individual responsibility must be absolute. A person's weaknesses and strengths, purity and impurity, are their own, not someone else's. They are created by themselves, not by others, and can only be changed by themselves, never by another person. Their condition is also their own, not someone else's. Their suffering and happiness come from within. As they think, so they are; as they continue to think, so they remain.

A strong person cannot help a weaker one unless that weaker person is willing to be helped, and even then, the weak person must become strong on their own; they must develop the strength they admire in another through their own efforts. No one but themselves can change their condition.

People have often thought and said, "Many people are slaves because one is an oppressor; let's hate the oppressor." However, there is now a growing tendency among some to reverse this judgment and say, "One person is an oppressor because many are slaves; let's despise the slaves."

The truth is that both oppressor and slave are cooperating in ignorance, and while they seem to harm each other, they are actually harming themselves. Perfect Knowledge understands the law at work in the weakness of the oppressed and the misused power of the oppressor; perfect Love, seeing the suffering that both states bring, condemns neither; perfect Compassion embraces both oppressor and oppressed.

Anyone who has conquered weakness and let go of all selfish thoughts belongs to neither oppressor nor oppressed. They are free.

A person can only rise, conquer, and achieve by lifting up their thoughts. They can only remain weak, miserable, and abject by refusing to lift their thoughts.

Before a person can achieve anything, even in worldly matters, they must raise their thoughts above base animal indulgence. To succeed, they may not need to give up all animality and selfishness, but they must at least sacrifice some of it. A person whose main focus is base indulgence cannot think clearly or plan methodically; they cannot find and develop their latent resources and will fail in any endeavor. Without beginning to control their thoughts, they are not ready to control affairs or take on serious responsibilities. They are not fit to act independently and stand alone. But they are limited only by the thoughts they choose.

There can be no progress, no achievement without sacrifice, and a person's worldly success will be proportional to how much they sacrifice their confused animal thoughts and focus their mind on developing their plans, strengthening their resolve, and becoming more self-reliant. The higher they lift their thoughts, the more manly, upright, and righteous they become, and the greater their success, the more blessed and enduring their achievements will be.

The universe does not favor the greedy, the dishonest, and the vicious, although it may sometimes appear to do so on the surface; it helps the honest, the generous, and the virtuous. All the great Teachers throughout history have declared this in various ways, and to prove and know it, a person has only to persist in making themselves more and more virtuous by raising their thoughts.

Intellectual achievements result from thought dedicated to the pursuit of knowledge or the beautiful and true in life and nature. Such achievements may sometimes be associated with vanity and ambition, but they are not caused by those traits; they naturally result from long and arduous effort and pure and unselfish thoughts.

Spiritual achievements are the culmination of holy aspirations. A person who constantly thinks noble and lofty thoughts and focuses on all that is pure and unselfish will, as surely as the sun reaches its peak and the moon becomes full, become wise and noble in character and rise to a position of influence and blessedness.

Achievement, of any kind, is the crown of effort and the diadem of thought. With self-control, resolution, purity, righteousness, and well-directed thought, a person rises; with animality, indolence, impurity, corruption, and confused thoughts, a person falls.

A person may rise to great success in the world and even reach high spiritual levels, but they can also fall back into weakness and misery by allowing arrogant, selfish, and corrupt thoughts to take over.

Victories achieved through right thinking can only be maintained with vigilance. Many people give up when success seems assured and quickly fall back into failure.

All achievements, whether in business, intellectual pursuits, or spiritual growth, result from well-directed thought, are governed by the same law, and follow the same method; the only difference is in the goal.

Someone who wants to achieve little must sacrifice little; someone who wants to achieve much must sacrifice much; someone who wants to reach great heights must make great sacrifices.

Chapter 6
Visions and Als

Dreamers are the saviors of the world. Just as the visible world is supported by the invisible, so people, through all their struggles, sins, and mundane tasks, are nourished by the beautiful visions of their solitary dreamers. Humanity cannot forget its dreamers or let their ideals fade away; it lives through them, recognizing them as the realities that it will one day see and know.

Composers, sculptors, painters, poets, prophets, sages—these are the creators of the future world, the architects of heaven. The world is beautiful because they have lived; without them, working humanity would perish.

Anyone who holds onto a beautiful vision, a lofty ideal in their heart, will one day realize it. Columbus had a vision of another world, and he discovered it. Copernicus imagined a universe full of worlds, and he revealed it. Buddha envisioned a spiritual world of pure beauty and perfect peace, and he entered it.

Cherish your visions; cherish your ideals; cherish the music that stirs in your heart, the beauty that forms in your mind, the loveliness that wraps around your purest thoughts. From them will grow all delightful conditions, all heavenly environments. If you stay true to them, your world will be built from them.

To desire is to obtain; to aspire is to achieve. Should man's basest desires be fully satisfied while his purest aspirations starve? This is not the Law: such a situation can never exist. "Ask and receive."

Dream big dreams, and as you dream, so shall you become. Your Vision is the promise of what you shall one day be; your Ideal is the prophecy of what you shall finally reveal.

The greatest achievement was once a dream. The oak sleeps in the acorn; the bird waits in the egg; and in the highest vision of the soul, an awakening angel stirs. Dreams are the seeds of reality.

Your circumstances may be unfavorable, but they will not remain so if you see an Ideal and strive to reach it. You cannot change within and remain unchanged without. Here is a young man struggling with poverty and labor; confined to long hours in an unhealthy workshop; uneducated and lacking refinement. But he dreams of better things: intelligence, refinement, grace, and beauty. He mentally builds an ideal life; the vision of greater freedom and opportunity fills him. Unrest drives him to action, and he uses his spare time and resources, however small, to develop his latent powers. Soon, his mind changes so much that the workshop can no longer contain him. It becomes so out of tune with his mentality that it falls away like an old garment, and as new opportunities match his expanding abilities, he leaves it forever. Years later, this young man becomes a mature leader. He masters certain mental forces, wielding worldwide influence and nearly unmatched power. He holds great responsibilities, speaks, and changes lives. People hang on his words and reshape their characters. He becomes the central, luminous figure around which countless destinies revolve. He has realized his youthful Vision. He has become one with his Ideal.

And you, young reader, will realize the Vision of your heart, whether it is base or beautiful, or a mix of both, because you will always gravitate towards what you secretly love most. You will receive the exact results of your thoughts; you will earn exactly what you deserve. Whatever your current environment, you will fall, remain, or rise with your thoughts, Vision, and Ideal. You will become as small as your strongest desire or as great as your highest aspiration. In the beautiful words of Stanton Kirkham Davis, "You may be keeping accounts, and soon you will walk out of the door that seemed to be the barrier to your ideals, and find yourself before an audience—the pen still behind your ear, the ink stains on your fingers, and there and then you will pour out the torrent of your inspiration. You may be driving sheep, and you will wander into the city, wide-eyed; you will follow the spirit into the master's studio, and after a while, he will say, 'I have nothing more to teach you.' Now you have become the master, who dreamed of great things while driving sheep. You will set down the saw and the plane to take on the regeneration of the world."

The thoughtless, ignorant, and lazy see only the apparent effects and not the things themselves. They talk of luck, fortune, and chance. Seeing someone grow rich, they say, "How lucky he is!" Observing someone become intellectual, they exclaim, "How fortunate he is!" Noticing the saintly character and influence of another, they remark, "How chance favors him!" They don't see the trials, failures, and struggles these people have voluntarily faced to gain their experience; they don't know the sacrifices made, the undaunted efforts, and the faith exercised to overcome the seemingly impossible and realize their heart's Vision. They don't know the darkness and heartaches; they only see the light and joy and call it "luck." They don't see the long, arduous journey but only the pleasant goal and call it "good fortune." They don't understand the process, only the result, and call it chance.

In all human affairs, there are efforts and results, and the strength of the effort measures the result. Chance does not exist. Gifts, powers, and material, intellectual, and spiritual possessions are the fruits of effort; they are thoughts completed, goals achieved, and visions realized.

The Vision you glorify in your mind, the Ideal you hold in your heart—this you will build your life upon; this you will become.

Chapter 7
Serenity

Calmness of mind is one of the beautiful jewels of wisdom. It is the result of long and patient effort in self-control. Its presence indicates matured experience and a deeper knowledge of the laws and operations of thought.

A person becomes calm as they understand themselves as a being shaped by thought. This knowledge requires understanding others as being shaped by thought, too. As someone gains the right understanding and sees more clearly the connections of things through cause and effect, they stop fussing, fuming, worrying, and grieving, and instead remain poised, steadfast, and serene.

The calm person, having learned to control themselves, knows how to adapt to others. Others, in turn, respect their spiritual strength and feel they can learn from and rely on them. The more tranquil a person becomes, the greater their success, influence, and power for good. Even a regular businessperson will find their business prospering as they develop greater self-control and calmness, because people always prefer to deal with someone whose demeanor is steady and balanced.

The strong, calm person is always loved and respected. They are like a shade-giving tree in a thirsty land or a sheltering rock in a storm. Who doesn't love a calm heart and a sweet-tempered, balanced life? It doesn't matter whether it rains or shines, or what changes come to those with these blessings, for they are always sweet, serene, and calm. That exquisite balance of character, which we call serenity, is the final lesson of growth, the fruit of the soul. It is as precious as wisdom and more desirable than gold—yes, even fine gold. How insignificant mere money-seeking looks compared to a serene life—a life that lives in the ocean of Truth, beneath the waves, beyond the reach of tempests, in Eternal Calm!

How many people do we know who sour their lives, ruin all that is sweet and beautiful with explosive tempers, destroy their balance of character, and create bad blood! It is a question whether the majority of people do not ruin their lives and mar their happiness by lack of self-control. How few people do we meet in life who are well-balanced, who have that exquisite poise that is the hallmark of a developed character!

Yes, humanity surges with uncontrolled passion, is tumultuous with ungoverned grief, and is blown about by anxiety and doubt. Only the wise person, only one whose thoughts are controlled and purified, makes the winds and storms of the soul obey them.

Storm-tossed souls, wherever you may be, under whatever conditions you may live, know this: in the ocean of life, the isles of blessedness are smiling, and the sunny shore of your ideal awaits your arrival. Keep your hand firmly on the helm of thought. In the vessel of your soul lies the commanding Master; He only sleeps—awaken Him. Self-control is strength; right thought is mastery; calmness is power. Say to your heart, "Peace, be still!"

Thank You for Reading

Dear Reader,

We hope this timeless classic has sparked your imagination and enriched your literary journey. Now that you've turned the final page, we want to share a vision for the future of reading—one where every classic you've ever wanted to explore is at your fingertips, in a format that best suits your life.

We'd like to invite you to gain immediate, unlimited digital & audiobook access to hundreds of the most treasured literary classics ever written—along with the option to secure deluxe paperback, hardcover & box set editions at printing cost. Together, we can spark a new global literary renaissance alongside our small, independent publishing house called "The Library of Alexandria."

Thousands of years ago, the Library of Alexandria stood as a beacon of knowledge—until it was lost to history. We aim to reignite that spirit of preservation and discovery right now, in the modern age—only this time, it's accessible to all, in every language and every format.

Picture a world where every timeless classic, novel, poem, or philosophical treatise is not only available to read but also updated for today's readers—modernized, translated into any language or dialect, and ready to enjoy in any format you choose, whether that is in an eBook, audiobook, paperback, or deluxe hardcover & box set version a printing cost.

By joining our movement to rebuild the modern Library of Alexandria, you become part of an unprecedented mission to offer:

- **Unlimited Audiobook & eBook Access to the Greatest Classics of All Time**

  Instantly explore thousands of legendary works, from Plato and Shakespeare to Jane Austen and Leo Tolstoy. All are instantly ready to read or listen to, giving you a complete literary universe at your fingertips.

- **Paperback & Deluxe Editions at Printing Costs:**

  Purchase any title in a paperback, deluxe hardbound, or deluxe boxset edition at printing costs, shipped right to your doorstep. Curate your personal library of Alexandria with editions worthy of display—crafted to last, designed to captivate, and delivered straight to your door.

- **Modern translations for Contemporary Readers in all languages and dialects**

  Discover a vast selection of classics reimagined in clear, current language—no more struggling with outdated phrases or obscure references. Next to the original versions, we aim to offer translations in as many languages and dialects as possible.

  As we continue our translation efforts and add new languages, readers everywhere can connect with these works as if they were written today. By bridging linguistic divides, you're contributing to ensuring that these timeless stories become more meaningful, accessible, and inspiring for people across the globe.

- **Your Personal Library of Alexandria:**

  Over the months and years, you'll curate a unique physical archive of classics—each volume a testament to your taste, curiosity, and love of knowledge. It's not just about owning books—it's about curating a cultural legacy you'll cherish and pass down for generations to come.

- **Join a Global Literary Renaissance:**

  Your support fuels an ongoing mission: allowing us to reinvest in offering deluxe print editions (including special boxsets) at their true cost, broaden the range of available formats and translations, and extend the reach of these works to new audiences worldwide. By joining today, you're not just preserving a legacy of masterpieces; you set in motion a powerful wave of literary accessibility.

We are more than a publisher—we're a movement, and we can't do it alone. Your support lets us scale our mission, preserving and reimagining history's greatest works for tomorrow's readers.

Become a Torchbearer of knowledge.

Thank you for picking up this book and allowing us into your literary journey. As you turn the pages, know that you're part of something larger: a global effort to keep these stories alive, share their wisdom across borders and generations, and spark a true cultural revival for the modern era.

If this resonates with you—please consider taking the next step by visiting:

www.libraryofalexandria.com

With gratitude and a shared love of knowledge,

The Modern Library of Alexandria Team

Visit:

www.libraryofalexandria.com

Or scan the code below:

www.ingramcontent.com/pod-product-compliance
Lightning Source LLC
Chambersburg PA
CBHW011357010726
47494CB00008B/2350

* 9 7 8 1 8 0 6 2 9 7 2 3 8 *